Inside Me

ZOE HETHERSHAW

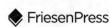 FriesenPress

One Printers Way
Altona, MB R0G 0B0
Canada

www.friesenpress.com

Copyright © 2022 by Zoe Hethershaw
First Edition — 2022

ISBN
978-1-03-913258-0 (Hardcover)
978-1-03-913257-3 (Paperback)
978-1-03-913259-7 (eBook)

1. *FICTION, FAMILY LIFE*

Distributed to the trade by The Ingram Book Company

Based on True Events

Introduction

I have changed the names of people in my story to protect their privacy, but by no means to take away the power or pain caused. The only name that has not been changed is my daughter's, as Maxie deserves a place of her own and never hidden. Her memory was always a painful one in my life, but now I'm free to love her for the true gift she was, no matter how short that was. As many parents that have gone through SIDS know, we have no answers to this, but we do have our story and one that plays in our heart like a never-ending tape recorder playing through all the wudda, cudda, and shudda moments, which in itself only leads to destruction. The gods of the medical field have no answers for us, so we tend to torment our own minds until we are finally healed through this horrific trauma.

This book will touch on many traumas that I have experienced throughout my life; I felt like I had a target on my back. But it is my story, and one that deserves to be talked about and also should be talked about. We meet many people throughout our lives; some are taken out and some are placed in. How this is controlled or what choices were made are a great mystery. I, for one, have looked back and often been amazed at this, and I am so thankful for not just the good but the bad also, as it truly made me the woman I am today.

I have been led down many dark roads and made many choices to go down those roads myself as well. If I have learned anything from my past and overcoming trauma, it is a fact that the past does not define us but rather refines us—providing we don't let it destroy us. Statistically, I should have never survived, but I did, and here I am, sharing with you all in hopes that you, too, will overcome. Or maybe there's someone you love whose behaviours you don't understand and maybe those behaviours are also because of the ashes of trauma; the house needs to burn down when the foundation is made from pain, hurt, rejection, betrayal, and abuse—how do you burn that house down? It's not easy and it's certainly not a weak choice. You may be ridiculed and lose people in your life, but what you gain is priceless. Be brave and know that even in the darkest moments that you really are never alone, and if you came through your past, too, I simply say welcome and well done.

Throughout history, we have tried to learn from our pasts, but does looking at our past or taking some good advice from our elders who have been through most of what we face today make sense to us? I heard years ago that sense is not common, so we must, sometimes, I believe, go through things on our own to discover where we went wrong or if the path taken leads to destruction or if it just leads to nowhere. Mine certainly led me to the unimaginable.

Some of the storyline is fictional—I'll let the reader decide—so here is my story.

Chapter One

I never really knew what love was or if I was worthy of such love. I hadn't realized how broken my heart truly was. This love will bring me back to life.

Everything will change on the day I receive a phone call; it will change me forever, putting back all my many broken pieces.

When my phone rings, it's a number I don't recognize, but it's local because it's a 604-area code.

"Hello?"

The voice is deep, almost hypnotic. "I'm looking for Nichole Shaw."

I reply with a curious, "Yes, this is she."

He says he is lawyer and he's been searching for me. "Why me?" I ask.

He says, "I have something that has been left to you by your father."

"By my father?" I blurt out. "I don't even know him."

This voice confirms my name again; then he tells me where I was born—Hope, British Columbia. He knows my mother's name, Ahava Shaw.

"And your father's name was Allan Shaw."

By now, I'm freaking out inside. I have only seen their names on my birth certificate; I have never heard anyone ever say them before.

I say frantically, "Yes. Yes. Yes."

This whole thing is weird, so I jump into asking him what he wants. He asks for my email so he can send me all the info, and then I am to contact him to set up an appointment to collect what is mine. What is mine? I think. He says my father has left me an inheritance.

I reply, emotionally wrecked, "Ok, ok, I will look it over."

As I wait for the email notification that will change my life, my mind is racing with thoughts. Maybe he was an Arabian prince, or a powerful man, then I think knowing my luck, he's probably just left me his debt. Arrrggg stop, mind—be still.

There it is—what do I do? How do I feel, opening something from my dad? Wait, my dad . . . Ok, this is really kicking in. Tears start drowning my cheeks, running down my neck. I don't have many memories of my dad. Mum died when I was five. No one told me about him; I thought he'd abandoned me. I never saw him after I lost them both that day.

I'm totally freaking out. I need to breathe. Voices inside are really not helping me. Ok, I can do this. How can this be that I finally get an email from him and when it's too late to even ask him myself why he didn't want me? Not even a letter or a birthday card to acknowledge my existence. He was alive, and I was the one that was dead to him. I am so angry, I need a drink, a large whiskey to calm my being. Then I'll open it and see what pathetic excuse he has to now waste my time. But wait, I still need to know what happened because I deserve to know the truth even if it hurts, so I open the email and there it is—a line with my name attached to his and there's a deep wanting and needing inside me that desires that attachment no matter how hard I fight it.

Inside Me

My Dearest Nichole,

I am sorry, I am only full of excuses of why I never came back for you and I broke my promise to you. I know there is nothing I can say now because you're reading this, which means I did not win my fight with cancer. I'm sorry I wasn't strong enough for that either. I tried many times to connect with you and I failed; you always looked so busy and distracted that I bailed out and could never just say 'Hi.' I watched you from afar and I was even in your favourite coffee shop one day just watching you in admiration of how beautiful you are. You are so much like your mother. I think that scared me. I am so sorry, this was not my plan. I planned to meet you and only wrote this letter as a backup, but I guess time ran out because here you are reading this without me. But know I am always with you, you are my daughter, my love.

I have prepared for you, though. I spent many years saving for you. I invested well so my gift to you is that you spend the rest of your life regretting nothing, trying everything, and fulfilling your dreams. I know I have no right to ask this, but I do have a condition attached.

I have enclosed a little black book. I want you to start with Mathew Fisher. He is my best friend. He's also a doctor, but that's not why you're contacting him. He will tell you about who I was. The book contains 12 people, some friends, some family, and only one enemy—sorry, but the truth is important. Mathew will give you the name of the next and so on. The last friend whom helped me the most is Lesous. He will give everything you need, including the keys to your kingdom. You are my daughter. I never left you, I always loved you. You have walked a hard life and my part in this didn't help, and this may not fill the void, but I will be looking down from heaven with your momma and we will always love you.

Your dad ❤

All I can say is—nothing, I have nothing to say. I am completely numb. My body feels like jelly, and my soul is crying out. I have pushed down every emotion for years. I have walked through hell on earth, and now—now I have hope, really. Do I trust hope? Can I trust hope or is this going to be another setback of running around after a man just to be hurt again? But, what if?

I have this small soft voice inside me so calmly saying, *I will walk this with you.* Ok, now I'm shaking. My entire being is collapsed on the floor, aching deep inside my chest where my heart used to be. Tears flowing. I never believed I could cry anymore but apparently, evidently, I am, and it feels so strange, so I tell myself, Ok, I will do this, and I will find my strength to walk this out, if only to see where this road leads. I will walk it out.

A walk—that's what I need to clear my head. Connecting to nature has always helped me breathe and gather my many thoughts, which can be a hard process, as there are so many voices running through it loudly, especially when old doors of the past open in my mind, awakening the sleepers trapped by trauma. I always thought everyone had the voices, as it's been as normal as I breathe air to me. It took me a long time to realize they came through the pains I endured at the hands of others, the ones that tried to break me and sadly succeeded. Even when I thought or believed I wasn't broken because I was alive, I was dead inside because of my many broken pieces. I can repress the memories but not my body ones; my body always remembers; it just doesn't connect all the pieces that my mind holds captive.

Remembering all the different diagnoses doctors have given me over the years, from schizophrenia to suppressed depression to multiple personality disorders, I guess everyone wants to know about the many voices or the hidden ghosts I have carried around with me or chased me. All I know is they're mainly all in a bad mood and most often just want to die because it's the only way to forget the constant pain and shame, but I can override them in many ways. One of the successful ways but most damaging is alcohol, binge drinking of any kind, and that's when they are all stacked against me and I have no choice but to give in when the feeling of anxiety gets more than I can bear.

Walks for me are good, especially whilst living in Vancouver down in English Bay, which is right by the ocean. I've always thought that I could live anywhere that was beautiful to see, and my apartment is so close to it. I'm on the fifth floor with an ocean view, but on some days, the smell of dead fish wafts through the breeze, reminding me that even this can be broken. Ok, ok, I can feel my chest tighten and my anxiety is taking over me—I need a drink, a large one. My mouth is like the Sahara Desert and my heart is racing and the thoughts of "just one drink, then go for a walk" overtake me. . . . I have an amazing collection of wine glasses and the large ones are my favourite; they resemble fancy fish bowls, which are great at measuring wine because half a bottle is one glass. The glass from last night is still half full; waste not want not, as the saying goes. I knock it back, drinking without thinking and praying that there are no fruit flies in it.

I'm searching for the bottle opener. I don't have a drinking problem. I'm fully aware that I have an escaping problem, and after the morning I've had, I need to escape and the only way I can in an instant is to forget and drink into oblivion. Grabbing the bottle and glass I head back to bed, just for a little while—well, that's what I think anyways.

*

The next morning is a perfect spring morning. I love the spring. The sun rises early as I stand staring at the sky with its most beautiful arrays of reds, oranges, and blues, above the roaring ocean with ships in the distance, mountains afar with snow tips, and cloud blankets wrapping them in beauty. This is my morning calm as I sip my sweetened, milky coffee, welcoming the calm before the storm. Everyday feels like a storm, one challenge after another. My mind is full of thoughts: some challenging but mostly negative, thoughts of past traumas and pains. I shake my head and say out loud, "No, not today." Today, I will choose to be in control and to not run back to my bed to hide under the blanket. Today will be different because today I have a challenge. Since the pandemic started, I decided to take a few weeks off work. My day job is working with clients with dementia, which I love because I can relate to their distortion in their minds, but I'm praying I never get it, as I have many timelines that I would not want to get stuck in ever. I guess time is on my hands and what a way to spend it, searching for the answers of my past and why I was abandoned? It's almost like it was planned in some weird cosmic way.

I make the call to the lawyer's office. A sweet voice answers with a greeting I'll soon hear so many times. "Gateways Offices, how may I direct your call?"

"Can you please put me through to Mr. Pathfree's office, please?" My heart is pounding. His secretary answers and we set up an appointment for today at 3:00 p.m. I'm not sure I could have waited even one more day.

"Thank you, ma'am. Do I need to bring anything with me?"

"Just yourself with picture ID, please."

Just myself, I think, and I laugh because now I'm in pieces. To bring myself, I may have to pull myself together, especially after only finding out yesterday that not only has my dad died, but he had thought of me. Maybe there's a glue for that, I think as I laugh. I reply, "Yes, ma'am, and see you at three."

I'm thoughtless and mind-clouded, having emotional rushes—anger, sadness, fear, uncertainty. What is this? I spent my whole life living in a box in my mind, and now it's like a huge explosion. I didn't light the match, but the dynamite ignited in my mind. Ok, breathe. I gotta get myself together. I'm gonna start with a shower. Yes, that's what I need. I can even smell me as I'm laughing at myself. Ok, what do I wear? Do I need to make a good impression? Wait, I'll have my power face on, and my clothes? Well, that's always a fight anyways; my mind says I look homeless no matter what I put on.

As I step in the shower, the water is hot as it's running down my bruised inside body, as I wash over my scars. A scar is how I'm feeling—it's a deep wound that's cut wide open and now I'm trying to heal it so fast I need the skin to layer faster, please. Inhaling the steam as I fight back the tears that I can feel building up from decades of pain, I think, Did he really believe I've had a good life? Wait, he said I walked a hard road. Ok, this isn't working. I need a drink.

I wipe the fogged mirror and see this clouded vision of someone I barely recognize. My eyes are so dark, almost black, which is the only feature I like about myself. Not true, I like my dimples, too, but now I'm laughing, as I resemble a panda, which reminds me I need new mascara. I'm gonna make this easy: black pants, black shirt, and white scarf, oh, and my comfy boots. I'll throw my hair up in a bun, and I'm good. My hair. I always wondered which parent I got my copper curly hair from. Whose eyes do I have? Did I inherit cancer too? Oh no, stop, mind, be still.

Ok, it's almost noon, whisky or wine? Wait no, one thing I have learned is not to drink when I'm going through something. I've had way too many bad days and many regrets. Besides, I'm in control and today; I'm gonna face it sober. I'll have eggs instead, scrambled—no, fried—yes, fried on top of buttered toast with salt and pepper.

I get into my old red banger of a car. Seriously, I don't think there's anything that doesn't need fixing. There's a faint smell between mould and cigarettes that always reminds me of an ole English pub. Laughing, I think, That's why I keep it. Who am I kidding? My car resembles me.

There it is. I've made it in one piece. I'm feeling really proud of myself; I arrived safely, even with the blackout moments, moments when I catch myself in a daydream or I lose time and don't quite remember the drive. Guess it would be worrisome if I had ever had an accident, but I guess parts of me take over and do life when I can't.

I'm here at 999 33rd Ave., just off 12th Street. I stare at the building: white-washed brick walls, with huge tinted windows. I swear it's like it reaches the sky. The red-doored entrance with a golden plaque catches my eye. I can't feel my legs; they're numb. My heart's racing and mind's flooding with so many voices, thoughts, and memories. I make it to the door, and I go in.

"Can I help you?"—the four little words from this sweet-voiced receptionist with black-framed glasses, her blond locks floating down her shoulders. Now, she is someone I would like to look like.

"Yes, please. I'm here for my three o'clock with Mr. Pathfree." Wow, I said it without stuttering.

"Go straight to the elevator and you will need the twelfth floor."

Ok, so far this is easy. As I get in and press twelve and the doors close, I can feel my entire body shrinking. Fear sweeps over me— can I do this? Can I really? What if he doesn't like me? Oh stop, this is not a date. As I chuckle to myself, I check myself out in the mirror, then shudder as I resemble a stranger. That's it—this was fast; I'm here.

Wow, it's amazing. I have never seen so much glass: glass desks, walls, windows. The walls are clouded and the light—so much light. I almost feel exposed. Oh my, there are flowers on every desk. White lilies, my favourite, I love them. My therapist thinks it's because I've had so much death in my life, but I disagree. To me, they're like purity and peace that's tangible to touch, but their delicacy gently leaves the evidence of a fine yellow powder, which I always get on my nose, so I will resist smelling them as I laugh.

"Can I help you?" Another one wanting to help me; words I would have done anything to hear growing up.

"Yes, please, I'm Nichole. I'm here to see Mr. Pathfree. I have a three o'clock."

As she smiles, I am mesmerized by her perfectly white glimmering teeth, her deep blue eyes, and amazing almost black curly hair—stunningly beautiful. Her desk says her name is Ariel. Even her name is amazing. As she guides me along the hallway, I notice her perfect hourglass body, thinking to myself that this woman definitely does not fight to get dressed. She smiles and ushers me in.

Mr. Pathfree stands and greets me with a handshake. His hair is like golden waves of sunshine and he has the lightest blue eyes I have ever seen. He smiles, and I feel drawn to him, not sexually attracted but drawn. He gets out a red folder, turns the computer screen towards me, and begins to talk. Ok, I have to be focused and really listen. In a soft voice, he says, "Call me Elias," and then begins to tell me all about this black book and a bank account opened in my name with a balance of ten million dollars.

Ok, I'm frozen. I don't think I heard him correctly. "Can you please repeat?"

He smiles and says, "Your father left you ten million dollars, and there is another signature needed by a gentleman by the name of Lesous."

He gives me a list of instructions, which he says my father's friend Mathew Fisher will walk through with me and he's already arranged to meet us here in about half an hour. The black book is light in weight and has an elastic band around it. I open it and have a peek inside. There's an introduction on the first page like a content page, a list of names.

1. Mathew Fisher
2. Maria Clements
3. Pete Clements
4. Andrew Clements
5. Josh Clements
6. Simon Walker
7. Mark O'Reilly
8. Gwenlynn O'Donnel
9. Ahava Shaw
10. Allan Shaw
11. Choshek
12. Lesous

I close the book. I don't understand what this all means; my parents' names are there. Wait, will I see where they're buried? Are they buried together? My mind is racing with many thoughts. Guess I should wait for instructions and not let my curiosity take a hold of me. Breathe, Nichole. Breathe. I have searched for answers for so many years and have come up with nothing and now I have too many questions and the main one is, who am I?

My mind goes silent. I think I'm in shock because I know I can think but I've never had such a silent mind. My body is slumped in the leather back chair, and I really need water thrown at me or something.

Then I think of how my life will really change and I'm not scared. I feel like I've been reborn.

Chapter Two

A knock on the door. Mr. Pathfree says, "Ah, Nichole, this will be Mathew right on time. Come in."

In walks my dad's best friend, Mathew Fisher. I first notice his bald head shining like a walking mirror, and his smile looks like he's going to suck me in. Oh, his eyes, he has the kindest eyes I have ever seen; they're like the Irish Sea green, deep with many stories and mysteries. His skin is like bronze, glowing and healthy, especially compared to my pasty, veiny, washed-out earth suit. He's wearing a dark blue pinstripe suit and his shirt is so crisp, white, with the first button undone. His shoes are like those fancy Italian designer ones; you know, the ones you don't see in stores, you just hear about their existence—ok, enough. I feel like I'm floating and must come back to earth.

He speaks, but I can't hear him. I'm simply mesmerized, and his lips are moving, but I can't hear what he's saying. I'm completely drawn in, knowing that this man knew my dad, was his best friend. I'm wondering if my dad was like him with fancy shoes. He is looking straight at me, and then repeats and I listen. I can now hear.

"Nichole, I'm Mathew, your dad's friend." His voice is deep and he's still smiling.

In my heart, I feel a deep sinking; my mind is racing with a million questions. I stutter back, "Hi," thinking, That's it; that's all I could blurt out. I truly am pathetic; no wonder I'm alone apart from the thousand friends in my head, who constantly do not shut up when I don't need them and are now silent when I could really use them.

Mr. Pathfree interrupts and I'm brought back down, like when you have that teacher at school that only needs to say three words, "Good morning, class," and the entire class halts and your sit there wondering, What is this one's power? I want that.

"Good afternoon, Mathew." Mr. Pathfree greets him like they know each other, and Mathew just smiles. Again, this guy smiles a lot. Maybe he wouldn't smile so much if he really knew me, which won't happen—nobody gets behind that wall.

Have you ever tried to pick a broken egg up with paper towel, its shell broken by a human and now there's this gooey mess? If you grab it just right, you can collect the whole egg, but you cannot put it back in the shell because it's broken, so it sits, developing a film over itself till it's hard again, creating a false shell. That's me. So yes, I have walls. Without walls and borders, I would be exposed. No one has ever tried to pick me up gently; they've just wanted to smear me, so I have learned to trust no one, have hope in nothing, and just exist, protecting my yoke. . . . Who am I kidding? That's outward talk. Inwardly, I'm desperately searching for the one to repair what was broken, even if only so I can breathe again.

Mr. Pathfree hands the red folder over to Mathew. I totally blank out through the conversation; I always do this and lose time. Oh well, I'm not going to ask them to repeat, as I want to look somewhat intelligent.

"Ok, Nichole, you ready?" says Mr. Smiles.

Of course I'm not, but I reply, "Yes, let's do this."

He smiles as he gets up to leave and goes over to give a man-hug to Mr. Pathfree, then turns to me with his hand outstretched to lift me out of the chair I appear to be glued to. He's smiling, and his lips are moving and I'm enchanted by the warmth coming from him, but I don't recognize it as a feeling. Emotions are definitely something I have spent my life trying to control, always believing that crying is a sign of weakness, and never vulnerable because that can only lead to death of oneself.

As we get outside, I can't recall how we got here, as it becomes a mere foggy memory. I hadn't even noticed who I saw on the way out because, as usual, my mind was racing with so many questions. I'm trying to focus and stay grounded. I'm trying so hard to catch glimpses of past tools I've learned to push everything down, thinking again, Whisky or wine? Then shaking my head *no*. Mathew looks at me with a smile and asks me, "Are you ok? This must be very strange for you." I respond with a forced smile, "I'm good, and yes, a little overwhelming." Who am I kidding? I'm a wreck.

He walks over to this really cool black retro car. This thing is older than me. As he opens the passenger door for me, I can smell the age of it—not like mould but more like old leather. I slump in the seat. As he puts the key in and turns it, I hear the lock and catch a glimpse of myself in the window. Reflecting the sun through me, all I'm seeing is a shadow image of myself. Now this would be a good way to stay, never seeing me, just an outline. I believe everyone does see me this way. Wow, you can smell the leather as I blend my black body sinking into the seat, a seat with many stories, I'm sure. It's just one long seat, no in-between. Oh, I do hope I don't slide into him—that would be my embarrassing luck. The beige dashboard, over-sized steering wheel, and even the radio look like the original. The roar of the engine is deafening but sexy.

"This car is amazing," I blurt out. "Where are we going?" I feel like I'm about five, like a child going for a car ride with my dad—oh my, where did that come from, and why am I so familiar and excited? This isn't my memory.

Mathew responds as we hit a red light. "We're heading to Hope. That is where it all began. Look in the glovebox. There's a gift for you from your dad."

Those words cut me deep. I'm not sure I'm ready for another surprise. "From my dad?" I gently whisper as I open the glovebox and see this red papered box. Placing it on my lap, I just stare, mesmerized by the written note.

Nichole, my love, this is for you to help you get through the next 12 days.

Love, your dad ❤

It feels now like a lead weight on my pencil thighs. The red string makes it tempting to pull. I'm still feeling like I'm a five-year-old version of myself with butterflies fluttering in my stomach, or is that because I need food? . . . Ok, here goes. . . . The box contains three envelopes, each with only a number written on them: 1, 2, and 3. . . . I open number one, which is the thickest. Wow, there's A LOT of hundred-dollar bills. . . . I'm sinking in my seat again and I'm losing my breath. . . . My mind's telling me there's a catch, shhh . . . The second envelope is a letter, handwritten. I scan to the bottom, which again says, "Love, your dad," breathe deep, and read. I'm not sure if I'm feeling lightheaded from all the deep breaths or the fact that I feel like someone has taken over my body. Ok, just read.

My sweet baby girl,

I want this gift to help you as a starting point to bring you to the truth of what happened. I've made sure you will not be on your own through this journey. Mathew is my trusted friend whom I trust to be with you today. I have hope that you will be able to see that you truly were so loved and never forgotten. Again I'm sorry I wasn't strong enough, but I hope the truth will shine light into our beginnings, when we were a family.

I've enclosed $3,000 to make this week fun also, so you can buy yourself a new outfit, have your hair done. You have your mum's hair, so if my memory serves me right, you have so many waves and curls. I often drift into thought that it shines like gold in the sun like hers did. She truly was so beautifully stunning, with a precious love that lured in the most broken of souls, my only love, and you were created from this love. You were so loved, treasured and admired; we always would dream of you being a world changer. Your mum's name was Ahava, which is Hebrew for Love, a name so suited, as if it was a gift from heaven itself as she was. Your name in Greek means victorious, which you are. Your path was a hard one, and you have done so well because you're here reading this.

Also eat at restaurants of your choosing. Mathew loves food, all food, ha ha. Your mum's favourite food was Italian and mine was sushi. As I'm remembering, your mum hated sushi. She always felt that something so slimy should never be a human right to eat, ha ha. And whatever else you need, my love.

The last envelope is the deed to a house in Hope. It was our home before the day that changed our lives forever. When you go in, you will see that time stood still. Nothing has been changed; everything is as it was. The housekeeper, Ana, is a beautiful lady and has kept the home well as her mother did before her. She will not be there whilst you are and this is why I needed Mathew to bring you there, because I am hoping memories will trigger. This car was ours. Your mum sat exactly where you are now and you were in the middle. Oh, how you loved changing the music, throwing your arms up and singing. I often imagine you singing on a stage somewhere. I remember the day your mum bought me this car, 1958 Impala. It was our baby before you and now it's yours. I hope you make many new memories as we did.

Be brave, my love, as I am always with you.
Love, your dad ❤

How can this be? I have seriously never felt so confused yet so calm. Most of the answers I needed through life have been answered in one letter, yet, of course, I have so many more. My foster parents, an endless supply, most of them should have been called prison wardens or they should be in a prison. Shaking my head, pulling myself away from those memories back to present, no one had any answers to where my real parents were and why they'd left me, and eventually I just stopped asking. Then I aged out of the system and didn't care anymore, but now I feel guilty for wishing they were dead. No, I didn't bring this curse on them. Oh no, I feel like I am gonna puke.

"Mathew, pull over."

He doesn't hesitate. I leap out the car over to a bush and dry heave, feeling the blood rushing to my head as I collapsed on the ground.

*

Waking up in a strange place is not something new to me, but it is something I have been working on with myself. Because it happens too often, it makes me feel like I want to die, planning the thoughts in my mind, so I am trying to build a better version than my younger me.

I am looking round the room. In front of the fireplace is some kind of creamy white animal rug, which looks so soft and inviting to lie on. I can picture a lit fire and me lying there feeling safe. The mantlepiece above is filled with family photos, in many different frames and sizes, and a huge family picture above it on the wall with a couple holding a baby. They look so happy, like those fake photos you get in picture frames when you first buy them.

In the corner next to it is a huge black box—it's a TV. I chuckle to myself. It is placed on top of a green chest, like an old ship, travelling chest—really wow, I'm amazed if it still works and what is that on top it? Looks like a DVD player but says VHS. Weird. On the other side of the mantle is a small slim wooden china cabinet filled with gold-trimmed plates on stands, matching cups and saucers, with a few photos there too. This couch is so comfy I have completely sunk into it. The glass coffee table has a '70s multi-coloured glass vase filled with fresh daisies and white lilies on it—you can smell a faint beauty coming from them—and there are little animal figurines placed around it. The room has wall-paper—nobody has wallpaper anymore. On the fireplace wall, the paper is light blue with little faded beige flowers, and cream with faint blue strips on the other walls.

I feel peace, like I imagined I would feel at my grandma's house if I had one. There's even an old musty smell. As I stretch my body out taking in a deep breath, Mr. Smiles walks in with, of course, a smile.

"Are you ok, Nichole?"

I don't remember ever being asked those words. I smile back and rush back to reality.

"Yes, but where am I?"

Oh my, firstly, I have never confessed that in fear of looking stupid for not remembering how I got there, and secondly, I'm smiling. Wait—this feels real; I'm not dreaming or hungover.

I can feel sadness coming from his posture as he sits in the white-washed wooden rocking chair next to me. He speaks in a deep voice, almost like a whisper, "This is your home. You are finally home. Before everything changed, this was a home made from love. It's like puzzle pieces have been missing, and now I am here to help you to bring those pieces back together again. It may not be complete, but you will see a clearer picture. Your dad wanted me to bring you to the beginning of where it all changed, almost thirty years ago now, to show you why he lost his strength and why his own shame and fears stopped him from seeing you."

My mind is racing. Looking back at the family picture, I'm now wondering if that was me, the baby cradled in her mummy's arms and her daddy standing behind them, holding them both so safely and tight. The mother's smile is slightly crooked, dimples and amazing teeth, deep dark glassy eyes and flowing curls of long hair. Daddy's muscular arms, strong shoulders—oh, his smile, it could draw in a million ships to sink into his lips—beautifully straight teeth, deep soulful eyes, square strong chin with a dividing line, like mine, shoulder-length dark curly hair. The photo is in black and white, so I can't see the colour, but the baby looks so calm and peaceful. It's me.

I hear a faint beeping sound.

"Coffee's ready. Milk, sugar?" says Mr. Smiles.

"Milky, one sugar, please." I smile. Smiling is becoming contagious for me around him. As he gets up from the rocking chair, my mind goes off again, wondering if that's where my mother sat with me, cradling me in front of a roaring fire, holding me, loving me; wondering if I was mesmerized by her beautiful smile or if I was nursed from her breast. Wait, can I allow my mind to flow towards love? Love is something I have no knowledge of; love comes with a price and pain. The first person to say they loved me was when I was a child; he lay next to me, stroking my face as his other hand was rubbing my thigh . . . Shake my head—no, not going there.

What time is it? Looking around, I see my phone. It's 6:30; no missed calls, no messages, nothing as usual. If I died today, who would even notice? Then walks in Mr. Smiles. I wonder if he would notice if I just crawled away and died somewhere. I sink further into the couch, stretching out to receive my coffee with a faint smile, and he says, "You are so much like your mum." Looking through his eyes, I can see a sadness. He gets out his phone and suggests we figure out somewhere to eat, as it's getting late. "Perfect, Nichole, I'll order for pick up and we can eat here if you want." Food—what is that? I just want a liquid diet right now consisting of lots of wine and a few shots of whiskey to start, and then a cloud to float away on, but I reply out politeness or from my guard, "Sure, Mathew, order whatever you like. I'm not fussy. But can we get some wine too?" I'm starting to feel comfortable with him even though my guard is up. I'm sober and my clothes are still on, so I'm doing good so far.

I sip my coffee, trying to gather my thoughts, trying to recollect what I was doing before the tornado of life hit me, smiling. I was contemplating ending it all; now I have a purpose; I'm not broke or lonely. If I run away right now, I have some cash, but where will I hide? Hiding from the world brought me to where I was; it's almost as if the cosmos knew this day would happen at the exact right time. I had wanted to join the cosmos, to be a star, drifting away in the deep, bouncing from planet to planet, but then even stars die.

I remember the only one in my life that I ever felt love from that didn't come with a painful price. Her name was Mary. She was my one; she was the one that wanted me. It was the system that wouldn't let her; they said I was her temporary because she was too old to adopt me. To me, she was a movie star because I had only seen people like her in movies. I got to be with her for I think three years before I was taken again. Apparently, they thought a group home was the best for me; they always thought they knew what was best for me. If I had to take a guess at what love was, I think I loved her. I found out years later that she had cancer, and that's why they took me. I only got to scream and throw stuff around; I never got to tell her how I truly felt; I couldn't put my feelings into words back then. Another tear falls down my cheek into my coffee. I think I've drank more tears than I've drank coffee. If someone collected them, there would be an ocean for sure.

A car pulls up outside; the slamming of a door, the creaking of a gate, and then the doorbell rings a sweet chime. I can hear Mr. Smiles's muffled voice. "Supper's here, Nichole. Would you like to eat at the table or stay where you are?" He is so caring of my needs—not used to this—I want desperately to move from this couch, as I do need to pee.

"I'll come to you. Just give me a minute. Where's the bathroom?" I leap up. Ooh, shouldn't have done that; I just got light-headed again.

"Down the hall, last door on the left."

I'm happy he's familiar with this house. I'm staggering down the hallway, looking for a light, feeling my way through, passing three doors till I hit the end. Ok, go back one. I reach in feeling around and find the switch, then quickly scan around the room. Pulling my pants down, I barely make it but I do. Under the large brick glass window is a beautiful cast iron slipper tub surrounded by old church candles. The walls around the tub are mirrored tiles, with a pink fluffy rug covering the wooden floor. Above the sink is a beautiful heart-shaped mirror with edgings in a broken sea glass mosaic. The light fixture is a miniature crystal chandelier. I love how it reflects rainbows on the walls, which are a dusty pink with beige flowers—wallpaper like the living room just a different backdrop colour. On the shelf above the sink, there is a small glass vase with three toothbrushes: pink, blue, and one with balloons on it, which is smaller than the others. That's mine—I'm thinking, Is it really? I don't remember. The soap is a heart-shaped and the facecloth lying over the sink matches the towel laid over the bath: cream white with light-pink flecks. On the wooden door is three dressing gowns; the larger ones are cream white and the smaller one is pink with a large rainbow on the back. In the corner above the bath hanging in a large lace basket is a large spider plant. It's so peaceful here. I start to imagine long baths, candles lit, and a glass of wine and soft music, the eminence of the candles reflecting on the mirrors. I wonder if I can, if Mr. Smiles wouldn't mind. Wait, is there a lock for the door? Yes, phew, I don't want to make that mistake again.

Walking through the hallway towards the light, heading towards the aroma of food, knowing my battle with food, which I don't want Mr. Smiles to see, I'm gonna have to push through this. My stomach is in knots, feeling full and tight, even a cracker would fill it. I can do this; I must show him I'm strong even if my body is weak. There he is, smiling as he's laying out a feast of pre-pared containers on a table built for six people. I can hardly see the table, just mountains of lasagne, burgers and fries, salads, steaks, mashed potatoes, veggies with gravies and cheese sauces—oh, and there's a couple of bottles of red; that's my focus, Shiraz and Cabernet, deep blooded, time for my transfusion. Ha ha. Rubbing his hands on a towel, smiling, he looks straight at me.

"I didn't know what you liked, so I ordered a bit of everything. Come sit, let's tuck in." As he pulls a chair out for me, handing me a napkin for my knee, I take a deep breath and reach out for a wine glass.

"Thank you, Mathew. Seriously, this is lovely."

He smiles and sits across from me. Everything is beautifully laid out. With a more serious look, he says, "I don't expect you to eat much. I'm sure you're feeling very drained. Just do what you can." Then he smiles. Oh good, he gave me an out; I grab some garden salad and a couple of pork ribs drenched in BBQ sauce. I pour another glass of Shiraz and delightfully smile back. "Cheers."

I wonder when we'll be leaving, as it's getting late. By the time we get back to Vancouver, I'll be asleep or passed out on wine; either way, I'm feeling pretty much like someone has taken over my body and put it in fight or flight mode. I must drink to fight this or I'll screw up again. Mr. Smiles certainly has done nothing wrong to deserve that part of me; my heart's racing and there's a hundred different scenarios flashing in my mind of past mistakes. The music playing in the background is actually quite calming, never been a classical music fan but always loved the piano. Breathe, smile, breathe. Focus on a tropical beach with no one there but me, lying in a hammock and a cool breeze whipping over. . . . Heart's calming down, breathing's controlled, back to earth I come.

As I leave the table and stagger back to the couch, all I can remember is Mr. Smiles standing over me, wondering if what I'm feeling is safe—that's all I remember before I'm out.

Chapter Three

Waking up is always a challenge, depending, of course, on where and, sadly, sometimes with who. Normally it takes me about half an hour and a coffee to come out from my very vivid dreams. The nightmares are worse; I certainly travel a lot in them and find myself in the strangest of places. But today is like déjà vu—almost like yesterday was a dream—but I know it's not because I'm on the same couch, in the same living room. Ooh, I smell coffee. There it is on the table next to me and the black book. I can also smell bacon filling up the air. I love bacon. I will even fail an eating disorder because of my love for bacon, I think, chuckling to myself.

I'm curious to see what's in that black book. Then Mr. Smiles walks in. "Good morning, beautiful. I've made bacon and egg sandwiches. Hope you don't mind white bread. It's all they had. Then I thought we would go straight to the first person in the black book to contact." As he's smiling, I'm thinking to myself, How did he know these are my favourite comfort foods? I reply with a shy smile and am barely able to look him in the eyes because he called me beautiful and I didn't do anything for him. "Yes, please, to everything you just said." He chuckles and heads for the kitchen. I feel so relaxed as I sip my perfectly made coffee.

As I breathe, calming my mind, I pick up the mysterious black book. Mr. Smiles returns and sits next to me. With a gentle voice, he says, "Pete and Maria—they're your first contact. Give them a call, and they'll meet you here. Are you ready to do this?" Their names are pretty normal. I reply with a false strength, "Yes, of course I am." I open the black book. It's like a diary—not that I would know, as I've never had a diary. My memories, thoughts, and feelings should never be read by anyone, I think to myself as I see the first page. It's handwritten just like the letters from my dad—wait, it is from my dad. I breathe deep and read.

My sweet Nichole,

I hope you had a wonderful evening and today we will start. The first ones you will meet are Pete and Maria. I won't say too much, as I want their visit with you to be special and in their words not mine. I am so thankful Mathew is with you, and be brave, my love, nothing but good can come out of this. You do deserve the truth. I am with you, watching you with your mum.

Love always, your dad ❤

There it is again, the phrase I would have done anything to hear while growing up and drowning. Wait, there's a number. Ok, I can do this. Staring at my phone, I'm thinking I want to bail, run away, scream into a pillow, pull all my hair out. Mathew interrupts my train of thought with a deep but soft tone and, of course, a smile. "Nichole, just text the number, 'Come over.' They're waiting for you. I'm not going to make you call them." He smiles again.

That's easier than he thinks, but I can do this. Besides, I want to know where I came from. Mr. Smiles is great but doesn't talk too much and I have so many questions that I want answers to, that I need to know. My stomach is churning; I need to eat this perfectly greasy sandwich. As I bite into it, the yoke breaks, dripping down my hand. That's it—my yoke's finally broke. It's running and exposed.

My phone vibrates. There's a response. I lick the yoke off my fingers as Mr. Smiles hands me a napkin, smiling again, of course. I feel a sense of peace. I didn't mess up; it's just a sandwich. As I smile inwardly to myself, a memory comes to mind: I was about seven years old, and it was about my ninth foster care placement in two years. The couple I was given to I believe hated me; any excuse to punish me verbally or physically, they waited for. I remember sitting on the floor eating a peanut butter and jam sandwich for my supper. Apparently, I ate too loud for them, so I was to sit on the floor under the table with their dog—or should I say, their baby—knowing if I made a sound, a kick could come from any angle.

I shake my head; no, I'm not there anymore. Breathe. Focusing back to present, I look at my phone and the reply says, "We're on our way, be there in an hour" and a smiley emoji.

"Wait, I'm not ready. I'm still wearing yesterday's clothes and, I'm sure, my panda eyes." Mathew laughs and calmly says, "Don't worry, I've put some new clothes in the bathroom for you, which I had my assistant bring over earlier. Enjoy the hot bath I already ran for you. Take your time." I leap up, grab my handbag, and run to the bathroom, thinking I shouldn't have got up so fast. As my blood is rushing around my body, my head is floating away and I hear a voice, *It's ok. You got this. Just breathe.* I'm not sure I understand this new voice; it sounds different from the rest, calm and reassuring. I breathe and slowly it works; I calm down.

I feel excited as I look at my new clothes: chocolate-coloured leggings and a long olive-green sweater. Oh my, it feels so soft, and stretchy. Good taste. Wow, it's cashmere. I've always dreamed about owning one of these. I've never had anyone buy me new clothes before, only underwear. I remember the first time I got a bra; I was eleven, I was in a group home. I remember feeling excited and uncomfortable at the same time. I'm shaking my head—I don't want to remember *that man*. I'm thankful this is just a sports bra and matching boxer shorts—some French name I've never heard of and both in black. Great, I don't think I could handle anything sexy.

I look at the bath, filled with bubbles and the whole room smells like lavender and vanilla. Now I'm floating but in a good way. Locking the door, making sure I'm safe, I undress, peeling away yesterday. If only my past could peel away so quickly. I choose the perfect playlist; music has healed and helped me so much, especially in my darkest days. As I press play and step into a cloud of bubbles, the song guides me through. Enya, "Only Time"—how appropriate, the first verse, "Who can say where the road goes or the day flows, only time." I close my eyes, lie back, and listen. My mind stills. My body relaxes and I drift away into an oasis of peace, to some far-away abandoned island.

I faintly hear the doorbell. Crap, they're here. I rush blindly to get dressed, making sure I'm somewhat dry, wetting my hair—back in a bun you go—and slapping on some makeup for my power face. There's a new toothbrush and paste. Oh good, my mouth smells like crap, I'm sure. Great first impression. Wait, it's not a job interview or a date. Breathe.

I can hear the door slam and "Where's my little Nikki?" Can she possibly be talking about me? I hate being called that, but it's actually kinda comforting too. As I walk down the hallway, feeling sheepish with a false strength, feeling like I'm dragging my body, this woman's smiling at me with tears in her eyes. She's beautiful, like a Spanish goddess, long brown hair creeping down her thighs with so many curls at the ends, perfect high cheek bones, deep dark eyes like mine. She's coming towards me; she has her arms open like she's going to hug me. I don't like hugs; it's my space, my bubble. She grabs me and squeezes; I think I'm gonna lose air. I hold my breath, my hands gripping my thighs in a clench. I exhale; I think I'm enjoying this, the warmth of her body. The smell of her perfume is like a mountain meadow, so fresh and clean. She kisses my cheek.

"I'm Maria, and I've sure missed you, my little Nikki. You're not so little anymore." She steps back and smiles, holding my shoulders. "Come, let's go sit, and this is Pete. He's my husband now."

As she walks to the living room chuckling away, Pete walks up and is about to hug me when Mr. Smiles pulls at his arm, pulling him back. They exchange a look. Then he just holds out a hand to shake. My entire being goes from stiff to jelly in seconds, thinking how Mr. Smiles has saved me, a feeling I don't have time to register. How did he know I don't like hugs, especially from men? Pete's hair is dark, black, curly, parted in the middle. As he smiles, I first notice the gap in his teeth, which kinda suits him, his crooked nose, and strong jaw, clean-shaven but with a shadow, and I can smell a wisp of cologne.

"Hey, Nichole, I'm so happy to see you again."

We head into the living room. I think they're waiting for me to sit, so I slide back into my safe spot on the sofa, forcing a smile as I gather my thoughts. Maria is just staring at me like I scored a home run. Mr. Smiles starts up offering coffee that he just made, and Pete offers to go with him to help. I'm thinking I don't need coffee, I need whiskey and lots of shots, please. I breathe deep and look into Maria's mesmerizing eyes, wondering if this woman knew my dad. In a beautiful soft voice, she says, "I can see so much of your mum in you and your dad. You have his eyes and your mum's beautiful hair." A tear runs down her cheek; she wipes it away with a smile.

I have nothing to say. My mind is filling up with so many questions. She knew my mum too? "It's ok, Nikki, I won't hurt you." She strokes my hand. Like I haven't heard that a million times before. I want to tell her to stop calling me Nikki, but I can't. She seems so nice and warm; I don't want to hurt her, so my mind must be still. I breathe deep. Coffee's here. Good, now I can have something in my hands and not my hair. As I sip, Mr. Smiles, smiling, starts talking.

"Thanks for coming. Nichole's had a pretty exhausting couple of days, I'm sure, so we'll take it gentle if that's ok with you two. We will keep to the subject at hand, as I'm sure there will be plenty of time to catch up later." Smiling, he hands me a letter. "Here, Nichole, this will explain everything in your dad's words." I reach out and grasp yet another letter, fighting back tears as I try to control myself. I don't want to show weakness. I open the envelope with a deep breath and read.

My sweet Nichole,

I'm sure this is overwhelming for you and somewhat exciting too. Remember I am always with you. Maria is my blood sister. Our parents were killed in a car accident when we were young. I am older, even though Maria likes to believe she is, ha ha. Mathew and Pete were in the group home with us in Manitoba. We all came to the West Coast together to start new lives. We always had each other's back and that's why they're the first to meet you. I want you to feel safe. They're the only people I trust with you and will only tell you the truth. Oh how I would have loved this not to be this way but it's too late now. Just know that I do love you and I never stopped. I just didn't know how to climb down from the mountain I created. Maria has a gift for you. I hope it brings you peace.

Always my love, your dad ❤

I'm staring into space, as memories are coming forth from behind an ancient locked door, thinking to myself, Is this why I feel so comfortable around them? I have an aunt, real blood. Oh my, I can't stop the flood of tears. My body's exploding as Maria cries into me, holding me so tight. "It's gonna be ok, baby girl. We have you now." Years of pain are washing away as I actually embrace this squeeze, falling into her like jelly, like a little child set free from a locked cell. My body's shaking as it's releasing, almost like scars are fading away; my bones feel like they're coming alive out of a bag. My soul's healing. I can feel anger leaving.

Then my mind is arguing with me, thoughts of this isn't real: she just wants the money your dad left you, she's manipulating you, remember this has happened before. I pull back, wiping my face, shaking my head back into reality, shock coming over me. She tries to grab me again, and I push her away. With a soft voice, she wipes away her tears and says, so comforting, "It's ok, Nichole. I'm here." My mind is in shock. She didn't shout at me or pinch me to behave; I need to think this one out. She reaches into her handbag and pulls out a little red box with a delicate bow and hands it to me. "This is for you, from your dad. Open it." I'm holding it, but I want to throw it down and run, but where will I run? I have nothing or no one to run to. I look over at Mr. Smiles; he's punching his chest with tears in his eyes, not smiles. "We're here for you." Taking a deep breath, I open it; there's a note.

Baby girl, this is yours. It's your mum's engagement ring and wedding band. They belong to you, tokens of our love, which is eternal. A love we share for you.

We do love you, ❤

As I gaze down at these two little rings, one of them is shooting rainbow light into my eyes, the delicate single diamond with two rubies and a band of gold. I feel like a river is crashing me against rocks. Breathe, breathe, breathe, taking a big gasp of air. Maria strokes my back.

"I remember the day your dad proposed to your mum, a private picnic, roses. Oh, there were so many roses of every colour scattered, making a path into the woods, till they came to this big flat rock by the river, where he had a huge bouquet of them in a crystal vase. He got down on one knee, but before he opened his mouth, your mum was screaming, 'Yes! Yes! Yes, I will marry you.' This was one of the happiest days of their lives. The second was when you came along. Your dad came over to see me and cried with joy when he announced Ahava, your mum, was pregnant with you." She's smiling as she goes silent into her mind with these memories. I know how that feels; there's always a body-sinking when you relive a good memory and a body tension when you relive a bad one. This was a good one for her. She takes a long gold chain from her neck, takes the rings and beads them onto the chain, then places them around my neck, smiling. "They are always close to you, close to your heart."

As I hold the rings, closing my eyes, I can see a memory, just a brief one of them both smiling at me. I feel comfort and safety. I think I'm starting to believe I was loved, but I don't feel ready yet, so changing the subject, I start asking questions. "So, Maria, do you have any kids?" She looks straight at Mathew. He closes his eyes and nods his head. She then responds, "Yes, I have two sons: Josh and Andrew." Then she puts her head down like in shame. I'm not understanding this, responding, "Cool, that means I have cousins." As I smile, I can feel my entire being get excited, but then she says, looking me in the eyes with tears filling up, "Not exactly. I thought this would be easier to say. Andrew is your brother, Nikki, he's your brother, not your cousin."

Chapter Four

"What? Did you just say I have brother? How do I have brother who is your son? That's sick. Are you saying you and my dad . . .? Your brother—my dad—had a baby together? Who are you?"

Maria jolts back to reply, "No, no, Nikki—"

Interrupting her, "Stop calling me Nikki. I hate that name," feeling rage building deep up inside me. They had a baby together, and now I find out. Why did they bring me here—wait, what kind of cult is this? Jumping up and running to the bathroom—I'm gonna be sick. As I fall to the floor lifting the toilet seat up in a position I am oh so familiar with, I start to dry heave, crying with rage; every fantasy story I held in my mind about my real family not abandoning me just got shattered in one sentence. I want to die, thoughts flooding in of how I could make that possible. Just end it, you'll be better off, no one cares for you. "Oh, shut up," I scream to my mind, then I hear Mr. Smiles.

"Nichole, it's me Mathew. Can you let me in?"

Jumping up, I unlock the door and hug him like a child. "How could they? How and why?" He holds me back and with a soft voice says, "Nichole, that's not what happened. Maria is not his real mother." I fall to the floor; he falls with me. "What do you mean?" I'm listening. Is it because I need to or want to? I'm not sure yet.

Rubbing my hair from my face gently, he says, "Nichole, I will only tell you the truth, as you're ready for it, I promise. Andrew was only a few weeks old when your dad wanted to take you and your mum for a drive. It was time away so you could feel special, but tragically it was icy and their car spun out of control. They didn't see the semitruck heading head on. The doctors said your mum died on impact and your dad was in a coma for six months, but you, Nichole, never had a scratch.

"Maria was babysitting Andrew. Nobody was thinking clearly that day. We all thought it best that you go with the children's ministry, as there was no other blood relatives, and we all thought it would only be for a short time and it would help take your mind off everything that was going on. Andrew was safe with Maria, and we all thought it would be difficult for her having you both. Days turned into weeks and weeks into months. When your dad finally woke up, he was devastated, confused, and in such a deep grief that he ran away. We couldn't find him for years, decades.

"He was so lost, Nichole. Then one day, he showed up like a new man. All he wanted to do was live again and correct the choices he'd made. It changed all of us and one of them was you; he wanted you to have what we have. Nichole, if we could all go back, we would have done it all differently. Please know this."

I'm listening, but it's not registering; I have more questions now than when I started. "Mathew, why didn't you just leave me alone? The darkness I knew was at least familiar. Now I know the truth—that no one wanted me. You came into my life and then you gave me hope again." He squeezes me tight in a hug I've never felt before. I start to melt and I can breathe again.

As my strength returns, I dry my face and neck. It's like a river has washed over me; I feel calm, but I snap back to reality and think I need to see Maria. Walking back into the living room, I see Pete holding Maria like a strong protector. She looks at me.

"I'm sorry, Maria. I should have let you explain. I have seen so many dark paths in my life and I've seen this before; I shouldn't have jumped in. I should have listened, so, please, I'm listening now." I sit back down next to her, Pete returns to his chair, and Mathew sits. Maria wipes her eyes, and with a stutter, she begins to tell me all about my brother and how she was so young when this happened.

"I knew you were safe, and I believed this would all end soon and my brother, your dad, would come home. Andrew was so tiny, but looking back, so were you. I am so sorry—if I could change it all, I would."

All I hear is *I knew you were safe*. Who lied to her? I wasn't safe at all. Bowing my head down in shame, I go into a memory: I was about five; I remember crying myself to sleep for what felt like eternity in a room filled with beds of all sizes, voices screaming at me to shut up or they'll give me something to cry for, which was in the form of a belt or a fist. I learned quickly not to cry. I learned my feelings didn't matter and my world was no longer safe. Then, coming back to present, I push back the memories. "So now what? What happens now?"

Mathew straightens his posture, grabs the black book, and hands it me. "Now it's time for the second page. It's time to meet your brother and cousin. Just text them; they're waiting in a nearby café. Maria and Pete will leave but you'll see them again. Ok, Nichole, are you ready?"

I'm starting to think this is a marathon, a race to the finish. Oh yeah, it is; I get paid at the end—yes, that's right—so I sit up straight and reply, "Yes, let's do this."

Maria and Pete grab their coats. Maria asks if she can give me a hug, which is fine, and gently whispers, "I'm sorry I forgot about you in my mind but never in my heart. I'm sorry I didn't fight for you." Once again, I feel the softness of her cheeks next to mine, and as we hug, her smell is so comforting. "See you soon, Nikki, sorry I mean, Nichole." Then they leave; Mathew is guiding them

out. I'm feeling guilty now for snapping at her—it's just a name—
and then shame washes over me, a familiar one that never seems
to leave me, but then I'm also feeling justified because she didn't
want me either—another to add to the endless line.

Mathew walks back in with a smile, of course, and he sits down.
"Nichole, I can only imagine how this must be for you, but I don't
know how you are feeling. I need to know if you're ok. If you want
to take a break, that's ok; this is about you, no one else."

Feeling comfort in his words, I believe he's being sincere. Of
course, I want to run away and hide under a rock or in some shady
bar somewhere to drink into oblivion, but I know that got me
nowhere, so knowing this is the path I must take for now, I reply,
"Honestly, I'm scared, but I also have this feeling inside of me I
want to explore more. You're right; I need the truth. I need to be
free from the gates of my past, so please let's do this."

As he smiles and nods, he responds in a deep soft tone,
"Remember, I'm here with you; you're not alone." I open the black
book and flip the page, taking in a deep breath like my life depends
on it.

My sweet brave baby girl,

*Oh, how I want to hold you right now, as tears are flood-
ing from my heart for you, also joy as you and Andrew
will be reunited again. It's been too long and that's my
fault, not anyone else's. Baby, I take full responsibility
and only want the best for you, but I also know you
deserve the truth. I am with you always.*

Love, your dad ❤

There's a number at the bottom.

Chapter Five

My phone beeps, notifying me of a message: "We're on our
way. See you in an hour." I don't recall messaging; I must
have lost time, something I'm so used to that it doesn't even
faze me anymore. Mathew walks in with lunch—bacon and egg
sandwiches again, just perfect. What's the time? It's 2:00 pm,
feels like years have just passed. As I bite into my sandwich and
sip my pomegranate juice, which I got excited about, thinking it
was wine, I continue to read Mathew, a tool I learned to protect
myself. He's so strong yet so soft; he has a peace surrounding him
that I'm not familiar with, so although I am still not trusting him
completely, I can feel a sense of being safe, not a caged safe but
safe like I'm in a meadow, running through wild flowers. It's weird,
but I am certainly willing to explore this feeling. So, I begin asking
him the one question that's been bothering me. "Mathew, can I
ask you something?"

"Of course." He smiles back. "I'm an open book."

Weird reply, I'm thinking, does this mean I can ask anything
or is it a mirrored response to get me to ask a question that gets
reflected to me? Had too many of those before; they only cause me
to close up.

"Mathew, you grew up in the system with my dad and aunt
but was my mum there too?" He puts his sandwich down, takes

a drink, swishing his mouth, and replies, "Yes, Nichole, we all met in the same group home, but your mum had been in the system since she was born. But that's all I know about her before we met; she never talked about it. I just figured it was because she didn't know any different, but a few years back, before you were born, your dad opened a memory door one night when we were discussing past pains. Your mum was contacted by her real birth mum just after you were born and she went to meet her. She was only fourteen when she had your mum. She thought she gave her baby up for adoption to a good home, but never knew her baby would spend her life in the system. It was very healing for your mum; she got a lot of closure, except this woman couldn't be involved in her life because she had a life that knew nothing of her past. I know your dad tried to find her again. He wanted her to know what happened, but we'll see, Nichole."

A tear falls down my cheek, knowing my mum had known what it was like not to be wanted and my dad too. I think that's enough questions for now; it can wait. "Thanks, Mathew, I'm happy you're here."

He gently reaches for my hand. "Nichole, I'm here for you. Anything you want to ask I am honoured to share with you. I won't leave you; you're family." Then the biggest smile I've ever seen from him appears. Pulling my hand back in defence, I reply, "I'm sorry, Mathew. I've never had family, or, should I say, remembered I had one. It's gonna take some getting used to; you see, I find it so hard to trust anyone."

I pull the sweater down my arm, covering up another scar, and the memory comes flooding in. I was fifteen when I ran away into a man's arms. He was so strong and handsome. He was twenty-nine, and I was needing rescuing. Little did I know at the time that I would need rescuing from the torture chamber he put me in for two years of my then-worthless life. But I survived, I got away. I smooth a hand over my stomach, remembering where my baby used to be, the first one to love me unconditionally but who also died. I can feel my body tense up with anger, sadness, and an overflow of emotions like a train wreck.

"I need the bathroom." I get up to leave and run to another safe room to cry. I walk into the wrong room. Shocked, I step back, looking around. There's a little bed filled with teddies and a bookshelf next to a rocking chair and a floor-to-wall dollhouse in the corner filled with Barbies; a fluffy pink carpet; pink wallpaper with creamy white clouds; pictures of my parents on the wall—oh my, this must be my room.

I sit down on the bed and reach for a bunny hidden under the pillow—I remember this, how do I remember this?—as I lie down on the tiny bed in the fetal position, closing my eyes, allowing myself to feel, my whole body goes from fight to rest mode. This feeling of being safe, feeling like nothing can hurt me, like the room itself is protected by some great force of light, with beams flooding through me, pulling down fortresses of steel walls. My body is remembering down to every cellular molecule, rerouting my DNA back to its original path of creation, like a rebirthing. My soul is crying out, like it's going to rip outside of me and then come back into me whole. I can feel a healing take place, and the voices inside are actually quieting down, like they're finally home. I fall into a sleep.

Awakened by the doorbell, I remember my brother is coming and must be here. I feel like I've thought this before, flashing back to a memory, just an image of my mother handing me a baby on this very bed to hold. A warmth fills me as I get up and rush to the door. My body's excited with anticipation—he's my brother, my blood, he's mine.

As I get closer to the door my body is starting to vibrate with excitement. Mathew says, "You open it, Nichole. This one's for you."

I swing the door open, and it slams against the door stopper, almost catching me back against my body. I see him—he looks just like my dad. He doesn't have longer wavy hair—it's short, dark, and straight—but his eyes and bone structure are the same. He smiles instantly and, wow, it's like light shoots out of his mouth, blinding me. He grabs me for a hug.

"Nichole, it's you, finally." His voice is so deep, and for some reason, I hug him like I've only ever seen in movies. I guess this would be the warm embrace. *This is my brother, this is my brother* is repeating in my mind as I smell his natural scent—no cologne, just him—he smells like home, if that makes any sense at all. I cannot put this feeling into words, but I know it has no triggers to memory, which I'm actually thankful for. I want nothing to hurt this moment—this hug feels like I just glued myself to him. This is my first hug that I willingly chose since I can remember.

Smiling, I joke, "Ok, let's unglue and go sit down. I have so much to listen to and ask." He smiles and we go into the living room. I offer him my safe spot on the sofa. He sits, and I sit next to him. Mathew says, "Hey, buddy, good to see you again." My brother smiles back. "Yes, Mathew, it is good."

It's almost like I don't need to speak; my soul seems to be communicating with his, as I can hear questions and answers going off in my mind. Then the doorbell rings again. "That'll be Josh; he was running late, as always." My brother chuckles. Mathew gets up to answer the door as I just sit, stare, and listen. I'm not going to let anything take this moment; I will protect this moment for as long as I can. Mathew introduces Josh as I scan him over. He's a little short and stumpy. As he takes off his baseball cap, I can see his hair is quite receded, but around his neck is curly locks of dark brown hair. His skin is olive toned, and his eyes are like a droopy hound dog's. He has huge lips, or maybe it's his beard covering them. Cute smile, though—oh wait, he's my cousin, my blood too. I then jump up to embrace him. He chuckles and says, "I'm guessing you're Nichole." Feeling a little embarrassed but more in a childlike, playful way, I smile. "Yes, I am she."

We all sit down; Mathew hands the conversation over to Andrew, my brother. "So, Andrew, why don't you start?"

Andrew looks all serious now. "Well, Nichole, a month ago, I had my world shocked too, so I can relate somewhat to how you must be feeling now. I thought Josh was my brother, which he is still is, by the way." He smiles over at Josh. "I thought my parents were my mum and dad. Turns out I was lied to, too, but after meeting everyone and hearing the truth, I get it. Don't still understand it, but I get it, why the decisions were made. I only met my dad—I mean—our dad once. I remember it really well. Mum—sorry, Aunt Maria—introduced him as her cousin. He took me to a hockey game in Vancouver. It was cool. I've played that memory over in my head so many times since then to understand the truth. They didn't tell me the truth because they said they were protecting me. I was a baby when it all happened. The best news, though, was that I have you, Nichole, my big sis. Now I'm not the eldest, ha ha."

The only thing that sticks in my mind is that he actually got to spend time with our dad. Why him and not me? Didn't he care? Was it because he was a boy? Oh, mind, shut up.

"Andrew, so you didn't know . . .? Wait, did you get the same deal as me with the black book?" He smiles and, looking content, responds, "I did, sis, but I can't share till you're done, then we can compare."

I'm thinking I won't share about the money, just in case I got more; after all, I'm the eldest—oh, mind, stop, I'm sure it doesn't matter.

"So, Josh, tell me about you, and I'm sorry I keep leaving you out." I smile towards him as he leans back in his chair.

"Well, cuz, it's certainly been eye-opening few weeks, a little earth shattering but also rebuilding. I now see life differently. Wait till you meet Lesous. He's amazing, and the party at the end. I'm grateful for this life-changing experience, and I wouldn't change a thing."

Ok, well, that didn't really answer any questions; if anything, it just gave me more. "Mathew, when do I get to meet Lesous?" Smiling back, he says, "All in good time, Nichole, all perfectly planned and timed. Anyways, I want to take you to your parents' room. There's something there for both of you. Come, come with me."

Andrew grabs my hand as I get up. "Let's do this together, sis."

I startle back. I have heard this once before, but it wasn't a good outcome, shaking my head, breathe . . . back to reality: this is my blood brother, not my past. I smile back. "Yes, together we can do this."

We walk into a red room. The walls are deep blood red, except one wall, which the bed is leaning on, that's a rich cream, with a picture of a field filled with wildflowers and one big tree, I think an oak tree. The duvet is deep red with cream floral imprints. There's a set of dark wood drawers and a matching vanity unit with a chair. On the vanity is perfume and what looks like a jewellery box, you know, like the ones with a dancing ballerina. Next to the bed is a nightstand with a brass lamp with stained glass, a book, tissues, and a small dish with earrings in it. There's an old chest at the end of the bed with a folded blanket on top. In the pictures on top of the drawers, my parents look so young and they're cuddling together under a waterfall, and lots of baby pictures—oh, I think they're of me, oh, and one of a little girl holding a baby. Oh, that must be Andrew and I. Oh my, this room is beautiful, even the old wooden floor with a sheepskin rug laid across; it is so unique and romantic.

Mathew goes over and opens the closet. It's filled with clothes, shoes at the bottom, and on the top shelf is boxes. He hands a red box to Andrew and me. "Here, this is for you to open together." I look at Andrew, my brother, my baby brother. "Let's sit on the bed and open it together." On the very top is a letter; of course, there is. I can feel the excitement exploding inside of me now, as I know it's from my dad, our dad. It reads:

My babies, you are now together. At long last, you are reunited. I know you're no longer babies, but in my mind, you will always be my babies, my loves. My heart is filling up knowing you're together for this. Also tears are flowing down my cheeks with joy. In this box is the deeds to another house; it's for both of you, so no matter what you will always have a home to come back to, and our memories will always be alive there for you. It's a house on Vancouver Island where we went on our honeymoon. I'm sure Mathew can help with the details. Please explore this room, we have nothing to hide from you, it was so filled with love. . . .

My body catches up with the words and some of the voices in my mind are saying, *We are free.* The chains that kept them captive are now falling off. I want this moment never to end. For the first time in my life, I feel safe. I can almost feel the memories of them in this room, where I felt loved, and I do not feel like I'm forgotten or yesterday's garbage; I feel alive, picturing the waterfall in my mind, a place of safety, a sanctuary somewhere to finally call home. I'm home.

Chapter Six

Time . . . time is an interesting concept. When I was young, I wanted it to go so fast, and then many times, I wanted it to not exist at all, and now I want time to stand still or to find that machine that will take me back, but then I feel like the voids in my life are somewhat being filled, like when you're in your worst moment and the darkness has you like a cocoon and you've surrendered to it but a single thought, a small distant voice, will cause you at the very last second to want to live, but you think it's too late. It's that moment that's helped me survive through this thing we call life.

I've always had a very vivid imagination. I believed I got lost in some mall and was away from my parents when some do-gooder found me and brought me to social services and I was just waiting for them to find me. After so many years, I felt abandoned and forgotten.

I look down at the scars on my wrist. I remember the moment like I'm watching it happen on TV to someone else; I remember the cool feel of release as life was passing through me, my whole body relaxing, but then just then, in a moment, I wanted to live—and now I have the scars as a reminder to kick back and fight. I'm now in that place again, but this time, I don't try to end my life. I'm feeling the same emotions through my body but instead it's like all the pain is leaving and the blanket that was placed over me is coming off and those concrete walls I built on the inside are crumbling. In this very moment, I can finally breathe without reminding myself to do so. I sip my now-cold coffee with a sense of peace washing over me, and I think I'm smiling; I feel like a child, one that I never got to be.

Andrew nudges me. "Hey, sis, how about when this is all over— this black book deal—how about me and you go check out the cabin together?"

As I feel my spirit re-enter my body in a jolt, I reply with excitement. "Absolutely, but wait, when will that be?"

Mathew interrupts, grabbing the black book and handing it to me. "Yes, good reminder to stay focused." Andrew chuckles. "Oh, Mathew, you don't normally need a cue to stay focused." Mathew, of course, smiles.

Looking at the remaining seven names, I wonder what else could possibly make my life change any more than it just did. "Ok, Mathew, who's next?" Mathew gets up to take the dishes to the kitchen. He looks at me for my cup, which I feel is glued to my hands in a comforting way as I do love cold coffee. "Simon and Mark; send them a message and ask them to meet us at the old bridge, if that's ok, Nichole? We're going to leave the house for this one." I feel a wall go up. I'm not sure I can move. As I calm my inner world with breathing, I reply, "Of course, let's do this and, Andrew, are you coming?"

He sits up to attention in his seat and replies, "Sorry, sis, this one is for you. I didn't understand this process either, but I'm so thankful I went through it. You'll be ok, and I'll be here when it's all over. We're tougher than you think, we have strong blood running through these veins, and when it's over you'll know why, just like I did." He gives me a hug, turns to Josh, and says, "Ok, cuz, it's time for us to leave."

If I could keep one moment frozen in time, it would be this one. I instantly feel bad because I never really spoke to Josh.

"Hey, Josh, sorry we didn't get the chance to speak. We will have another, I hope."

Josh sheepishly replies with those big hound-puppy eyes. "Of course, cuz, you're stuck with me now." As he chuckles loudly, Andrew pipes up. "Cuz, come on, don't torture her thoughts with that idea."

Little does he know that for the first time in a long time, this could never torture my thoughts. My own mind is already tortured with the mountains of memories that keep it in chains. After I think about this for the first time, I actually wonder why I thought this. Shaking my head, I smile back and reply, "I welcome the challenge."

As they are leaving, I feel a deep pull from within to ask them to stay, but I know—and I don't know how I know but I know—I will see them again soon. Wait, Andrew mentioned a party at the end. My body now relaxes with hope. As I hear the laughter end in the hallway and the door close, I reach for my phone and message Simon and Mark to meet us at the old bridge. What am I going to see? I imagine an old bridge like the one in a movie I watched when I was young and think I may need a drink for this one. Then I realize that I haven't needed a drink for a while. I'm really not used to meeting new people; I've kept myself closed off for so long, protecting myself, which I work at because it's almost like I attract trauma just by being alive.

My phone beeps. I have a reply. "We will be there in one hour, see you soon."

My body jolts back into a memory—a date I went on, with the same message reply; I remember vaguely the place he took me to. We'd had so many vodka shots I only have flashbacks and then waking up in some seedy motel room alone. My body tenses, feeling violated and disgusted. I get up to go to the kitchen. I know there's wine here somewhere. I scan the counters; next to the cookie jar and olive oil is a bottle of red calling my name, no it's a cork top—where's the corkscrew? Rummaging through the drawers, I find one. As the cork pops, I feel a presence behind me. Mathew is standing there smiling. "Let me help you with that." He reaches into the cupboard and places a glass on the counter, then takes the wine and starts to pour. I'm thinking, He better pour all the way to the top—don't be tight—and then I'm thinking that he's not judging me. I ask him, "Why are you not judging me?" He replies with a serious look, not one I've seen on him yet, "Nichole, life has taught me to meet everyone where they're at. Don't worry, I will drive us, and if you want to cancel, we can do that too. It's really not a big deal."

Propounded by his response, I pick up the glass, staring at the red liquid. It's like blood mixed with water. Many times, I have wanted this in an IV going straight into my veins, taking away my pain, calming my mind, relaxing my body, and taking me to another planet entirely. As I go to chug it down, thoughts flood my mind, *You will feel better when you do; it's just one drink, then another one.* Then comes a thought: *Do I need this?* A challenging thought I'm unfamiliar with, then another, *It's ok; it's just one drink; you'll be fine.* My mind is racing and arguing with me. I put the glass down and say, "Actually, Mathew, I'll be fine. This one can gather fruit flies." I chuckle to myself, and of course, Mathew just smiles.

"Let's go, Nichole, it's a bit of a drive but a beautiful one, one of your mum's favourites."

As I grab my sweater, I say, "I'll just go and freshen up first; then I'm ready."

As we leave, I'm looking back at my home, a place I never chose to leave, but I am so thankful I could return. I try to look ahead to see if there are any triggers of memories through the streets surrounded with trees and mountains, hugging this small place like a blanket.

We pull up to a restaurant. Mathew says with a smile, "I ordered us some food to go, as I'm not sure how long we will be. Burger and fries. I also asked for bacon and cheese on yours. Hope that's ok. Would you like an iced tea?"

"Thank you, Mathew, and yes, you truly are so considerate and think of everything."

As he goes into a friendly family-style place, I go through my phone, looking at old messages. Well, they feel old and so distant now, yet they're from last week. There it is—the name I renamed as *asshole*, someone whose actual name has no relevance in my life anymore. He was like an addiction, one that you need help breaking or think you do. I thought I loved him, but for some reason, as I look for love from him in our desperate messages, I suddenly feel a goodbye. I'm not getting the usual emotions of loss, grief, anger, rejection, just a sense of peace to let go and it feels ok to let go. I type a final message: "Hey, I just wanted to say I hear you. I finally hear what you've been trying to tell me, so I want to say sorry, sorry for stalking you and I'm sorry for not letting you go, so I'm setting you free and me free to be who we're supposed to be. I want only the best for you and your future. Goodbye, old friend." As I click send, I feel like a piece of me has returned to my body, healed. Now I will delete and block—this deserves no more communication. I feel a sense of strength, like taking my power back.

Then the door goes and the smell of food fills the air—vinegar, fries, bacon, and melted cheese—oh my, I hadn't realize how hungry I am. I search the bag Mathew gives me and eat like my life depends on it.

Time is going so fast. I look up and open my eyes. I see a bridge. Chewing the last of the fries, sipping the ice-cold, sweet drink, there it is—a bridge. It certainly looks old, so I guess this must be the old bridge. It has a wooden frame, which looks like an ancient door leading into the forest, like something out of a story, water gushing under it, crashing the rocks, which are perfectly guiding it. Mathew asks for my garbage and says, "We're here, Nichole. Are you ready?"

I am so relaxed, surrounded with safety. I reply, "Thank you, Mathew, for being with me through this. I can kinda see why you were chosen, so thank you, and yes, let's do this. Wait, who are they? The black book had no letter or notes to read."

He grabs my hand and, with a low tone in his voice, replies, "That's because we're at the place everything changed, and this piece of the puzzle needs to come from the source of that day."

As my body tries to go into defensive mode, I'm fighting it because I need this—I need the truth and I need to be free from this pain. As I get out of the car, I turn to Mathew. "Come on, Mathew, please, let's do this." He gets out, comes over to me, grabs my shoulders, and, looking straight into my eyes, says, "Nichole, I need you to open your heart and listen. This may have been the event that happened that day, but it is not the cause of all the pain. Please remember that." As he rubs my shoulders, I can feel my body ease up; my body trusts him; he's not a threat. I guess this is how you are supposed to feel around a normal family that hasn't hurt you. I close my eyes, taking in a deep breath, and breathe out—ok, that didn't work, so I do it again and again—now my body and soul are relaxing. I open my eyes, look into Mathew's, and smile. "Ok, an open heart, you say. I can only try."

Mathew smiles and responds, "I only want you to try because I know it's worth the try."

I lean closer to him and have a weird urge to hug him, so I surrender and give in and I don't care if he pushes me away; I need this. He just puts his arms around my withered little bony body and I can breathe again.

Just then I see a car pull up next to us, and two men get out. The one getting out the passenger door has a rugged look, you know, like the old bikers with their long beards but shaven cheeks, salt and pepper wispy hair to his shoulders, jeans, white T-shirt with a leather vest. I'm thinking his hair needs a cut so he can go bald gracefully. He carries a sadness about him as he walks towards us, looking at the ground. I can't see his eyes; I always need to see people's eyes; it helps me see if they're alive or soulless. The other man, who was driving, looks like he goes to church: clean shaven, smartly dressed in a checkered shirt tucked into his jeans. His hair is dirty blond, neatly cut, and as he looks at me, his eyes shine. They appear dark brown but are like mirrors, like light is shining from them, like they could read my soul.

Mathew greets them with a hug and smile, of course, and then they raise a hand out to me and greet me, the biker guy first.

"Hey, Nichole, I'm Simon. It's my pleasure to finally meet you." His eyes are a deep green, like the emerald sea, filled with stories and treasures you could drown in. Then the church guy stretches out his hand.

"Me too, Nichole. I'm Mark. It's also my pleasure to finally meet you."

They both appear to be safe enough; besides, I have Mathew. I feel like I'm just following; my mind is floating instead of its usual arguing self, it's just floating, but my body is stiff. It's a struggle to put each step forward, and my hands are in the protection of my pockets.

A memory comes back from when I was around eleven. I was just walking to the store with my hands in my pockets, contemplating why I was alive, and then one of the kids nearby ran up behind me and pushed me. Because my hands were in my pockets, I hit the pavement straight onto my face and knocked myself out. When I awoke, there was about three kids around me laughing; I don't know why they were laughing; I just remember that I wanted to die more in that moment than any other. Shaking my head back to reality, I quickly pull my hands out and listen to the water gushing under the wooden planked bridge, taking in the fresh pine air with a floral hint from the wildflowers. In this moment, I can breathe. Nature is always my friend and can always bring me back. I believe it's because I can control this environment; it doesn't contain a soul to hurt me; its intention is not to hurt me; in this place, I'm in control.

As we reach the end of the bridge, I tune into their conversation about trees or something, I don't know; it comes to an end, and honestly, I don't think I missed a thing.

There's a bench we can sit on—oh, I do hope we're going to sit, as my scrawny legs are not used to long walks; certainly a hike is not in order. My mind is racing with thoughts of who these two are; then I remember that one of the people I'm to meet is an enemy. What does that even mean?

Mathew reaches his arm out, pointing to the table. "Let's sit here."

It's almost like he can read my mind; what kind of a doctor is he anyways, and why does he not ask any questions about who I am? Oh, stop it and breathe, breathe away and shake it off.

I sit next to Mathew so the two men can sit on the other side together. This bench is amazing; it's made out of logs. The bench seat is a tree cut in half, but it looks like it has been painted with too much varnish—ok, focus, I need to keep my mind in the now. The biker guy puts a soft red leather briefcase on the table. Mathew asks him to start, and as he takes in a deep breath, I'm thinking that this guy has a lot to say because he breathes like I do. Breathing deep helps me to gather my thoughts and calms my mind. Then he pushes the briefcase towards me and says, "Nichole, everything you need is in here. I'm the guy that called the ambulance and pulled you and your dad out of the car." Then he looks down with sadness. "But I couldn't get your mum. I'm so sorry; I hope you can forgive me."

My entire body is vibrating like it's remembering. I get a memory, a brief one in my mind, but I can't see his face; I just feel like I'm being pulled and my legs are stuck. As the man is tugging me, my leg frees, I am put on the grass, and the memory fades again—but, wait, I was told she died on impact.

"Simon, there's nothing you could have done. My mum died on impact, that means she wasn't even breathing. Why do you carry this pain when it wasn't your fault?"

Mathew smiles at me as Simon's eyes start to fill with tears. "Nichole, even though I know this in my heart, my head won't let go. Your dad was so gracious to me and helped me throw away the booze I used to bury the guilt and my shame. Three years ago now. It was so much for my mind to comprehend. I'm still healing, but I thank you, Nichole, truly I thank you for releasing me."

Then I notice him take in a deep breath and release. He looks me straight in the eyes with a smile, not a happy smile, but more of a I'm-gonna-get-through-this grin. I reach out to hold his hand.

"Simon, of course I forgive you, but honestly there's nothing to forgive. If anything, there's everything I need to thank you for. You got me out, and even though my life's been a rollercoaster of pain, I honestly don't hold anything towards you. I don't even know you, yet I feel nothing but gratitude, so thank you, Simon. Thank you."

Do I actually believe what I just said? My mind is arguing that he is the enemy because if he had left me there to die, I wouldn't have been begging to die till now. Oh, this hurts—why didn't I have that drink?

Then Mark jumps on the conversation. "Nichole, there's no easy way to say this. I'm the driver of the semitruck that collided with the vehicle that day. I had soft wood, which weighed in at

34,000 pounds. I'm so sorry I was on the road that day. I saw your parents' car spin out of control, and before I knew it, we collided. It's impossible to break hard on those trucks; I haven't driven one since. I too met with your dad three years ago. I was angry for such a long time. I was angry at myself for not being able to be in control; it haunted me for what happened. I even went to see your dad in the hospital and told him my pain, but he was in a coma and it wasn't till I met him that I knew that he heard me that day. He could hear everything I said. He only had forgiveness and was actually happy to see me. I didn't understand why, and he has forever changed my life. Learning his story strengthened me and meeting Lesous through him? Well, I know I can't tell you about him as you will meet him yourself, but I want you to know, Nichole, your dad was an amazing man. He had such a journey to get to where he did and you'll learn about that too, but I am truly blessed to know him."

I think I'm frozen, actually frozen. I can't speak, feel, or even think; I don't remember anything and that frustrates me. I feel Mathew putting his arm around my shoulders and pulling me in towards himself. I'm stiff like a board, and then he whispers, "Love will heal you, Nichole. Forgive yourself for holding onto your pain," and then he kisses my hand. Forgive myself? Really? I did nothing wrong—what a stupid thing to say. I pull away from him.

I thank Simon for sharing. I ask if we can leave now. I don't feel safe, I feel cornered, I need to feel safe, I need to numb all these feelings, my body is in flight mode, and my mind is in fight mode. I must have a whiskey or something stronger; I can't handle this. Simon and Mark stay at the bench as Mathew follows me to the car. I grabbed the briefcase and fled before I said something that I couldn't take back. My blood feels like it's boiling, my heart's racing; why do I feel like this? I am so angry, I want to kill something or someone. Why did my dad forgive him? He had no right to do that; if he wasn't on the road, my mum would still be here and I would have not gone through the hell I did. How dare he, I hate him and I hate myself, I want to kill myself—yes, that's the answer; I can do that. Wait, I can't do that; I can't even get that right. Then I think of Andrew, my brother. No, I can't do that. I need to stay strong for him; I can't lose him again. I get into the car, clenching the briefcase, angry at what Mathew just said to me and insisting in my mind that I have a right to feel this way. After all, he knows nothing about me, absolutely nothing—how dare he.

As he gets into the car, grabbing his seat belt, he says, "I'll drive you home, and I'm so sorry, Nichole." In my anger, I blurt out, "Yes, take me home. I want to go back to Vancouver, not that house. That's not my home. I have a home. Take me back now, please."

"Of course, and is there anything I can give you?" He reaches into the backseat and grabs a black medical briefcase. He opens it and pulls out a medicine bottle with a smiley face on it. "Nichole, here, please take two of these. They will help to calm you down, relax you. I'm not asking you; I'm telling you to do this."

I am thrown back with this, as I've never seen this side of him, but, wait, he's a doctor. I may not trust him right now, but I do trust pills. Then a small soft voice tells me that it's ok to feel afraid, just trust the process, and Mathew is not the enemy—*it's just that you're not used to the truth and you're frightened. But it's ok. You are ok.* I take a deep breath in now, but I still want to escape, so I look now sheepishly at Mathew and say, "Ok, fine, I'll take them, and thank you. I truly am so sorry for my behaviour."

As he hands me the pills, I'm thinking, Oh I remember you, two little pink pills, my seras. I throw them back and chug down the remaining sweet tea. Now breathe. Breathe. BREATHE.

Chapter Seven

Normal, what is normal? For me, normal is waking up and taking at least half an hour to understand my surroundings, find my safe voice, and come out of whatever dream I was in. Normal is a lack of trust in humanity and certainly in love. Normal is striving everyday just to be alive; normal is making every breath count and mean something; normal is finding a purpose to live in every moment. Normal, what is normal anyways? Are we not all running from something or to something?

As I awaken, I find myself struggling to differentiate between what was dream and what was reality. Collecting all my inner beings from whatever flight they were on. Calming the thoughts and putting everything back into comfortable boxes like filing cabinets in the vast library in my mind. Some thoughts which I dare to embrace in that moment can be knocked away with the shaking of my head or having to say aloud, "No, not today." Locking them away for another day, another year, or even trying to erase them, which, by the way, never happens; I am in denial—no, I don't believe so—I'm just not in a place where that could be possible. That's the thing with trauma, it becomes a friend you can never get rid of; it just lingers in the mist of my existence, waiting to be heard and trying to repeat itself if given the chance, then comes the forever-distracting thought of "I need coffee" and that thought takes over my mind to be the focus, the escape—yes, we'll call it an escape because now I just need coffee and music or some kind of noise to distract the quiet and then everything will be ok.

Now I'm remembering the actions of yesterday: how I humiliated myself, my out-of-control behaviour. Why did I react so harshly to Mathew? He is so nice and kind; I'm sure he just means well. Why am I so destructive? How can I run away and not have to deal with the once again endless apologies for my behaviour? Is he still here or did he run like he should? Anyone who tries to get close to me when they actually find out the real me always runs, so shut up and remember today is about surviving not striving. If he left me, so what, I don't care, but wait—I do care. Oh, I need coffee. Wait, where am I? Oh my god, this room is so familiar. It's my parents' room; I'm in their bed; how did I get here? Why did I get here? As I leap out of the bed, my body is shaking off the thought of sleeping where dead people did; then I quickly remember and feel bad because they were my parents. Oh my, they had sex in this bed—yuk, oh stop—why do I do this? I shake my head, bringing my thoughts under some kind of control, realizing I need the bathroom.

Opening the bedroom door like I've broke into this place and need to escape quietly, I peek my head out to look and hear from the hallway if anyone's here or if I'll get caught. My heart is racing with fear; I smell bacon and coffee; I hear the radio playing; it's coming from the kitchen. I tiptoe to the bathroom, hoping I'm not found, knowing the bathroom door and floorboards creak like a haunted house. I quickly shut the door, lean against it and breathe, thinking that the world must be deaf to my very existence. I'm feeling groggy—oh yeah, those pills I had; they must have knocked me out. I know Mathew is in the kitchen because of the bacon, which makes me smile to think I know him from that smell, but I guess I've had memories form from much worse smells. I am feeling grateful that he didn't run away from me—not this time anyways—but also angry. Why didn't he take me home? Am I really his hostage here? Is the money really worth all this pain?

I'm not feeling better, I'm feeling worse, like my entire being is being ripped out of my body and laid bare on the floor for all to stare and laugh at. I need my own bed; I need to hide and feel safe. How can I get escape and run home? Oh wait, I have the money my dad gave me—that should easily pay for a cab and I'll still have enough left over to get wasted. I need to die so this whole nightmare will be over; like I care anyways. Where I came from, it's not like anyone ever cared for me.

I look in the mirror, and what do I see but a strange, familiar face staring back at me as I chuckle to myself. My eyes are sunken in from all the damage, the layers of scars surrounding them. A scar rests on the bridge of my nose. I remember that night well: I was asleep when I woke up to him on top of me, pushing a knife down on it. I asked what he was doing; he said he just wanted to see how quick it would bleed. I pleaded with him to stop and he did; then he took what he wanted as I left my body—seeing the scene from above, just waiting for it to be over—and then I cried inside, scared to fall asleep; I was always scared to sleep from waking with the sound of a man sneaking into my room, pulling down my pants to look at me—he never touched just looked. I would pretend to be asleep, dying inside—ok, enough, mind, be still. I shake my head, then wash my face with cold water to shock it into reality; it feels like forever since I bathed, which is normal, as it doesn't matter how clean I am, I'm always dirty. I'll take a bath and maybe drown in it, hopefully; that seems more likely than trying to get home. I start to run the bath, pouring in the lavender and vanilla oil, instantly smelling the sweet fragrance. My baths are always really hot; I guess it's to try and clean me—like that will work. I'm gonna go and see if there are clothes that fit me in the closet, and I'm sure my mum wouldn't mind.

Dresses, so many dresses. They're long, which is good, but why so many? I hate floral patterns; they make the people wearing them look happy. Ok, I'll try this; I'll make myself look happy. Why not? I've pretended at everything else I'm my life, to dress invisible; why not try this? As I look at this beautiful deep red dress filled with black roses, it mesmerizes me. I can see me wearing this walking along the beach at sunset. Maybe if my daughter had lived, I could have been the mum to wear these dresses, and she would have loved me unconditionally. I feel my heart harden again, pushing down that pain. Grab the dress and search for underwear. Growing up in group homes, we shared everything, so this shouldn't be a problem. The first drawer I open, I find a whole stack of—oh my—they're granny knickers. Oh, this will be fun; no string backs, but then again at least I won't get weirded out wearing these. And a stack of leggings—even better. You're amazing, Mum; I can feel comfortable now with these under my dress. Better check on the bath.

Ok, I'm all set. The room is like a sauna and a field of flowers— what a perfect combination. I guess I should go and face Mathew first and see if he even wants to speak to me. Besides, I don't care. I still need coffee, and I still want to run away.

"Good morning, Nichole." He greets me with a smile as he hands me my sweetened coffee. "I made you bacon." He smiles again. Did he forget yesterday? Did he forget how rude I was to him, and how mean he was to me? Maybe he enjoys the behaviour, I dunno, but what I do know is my heart just relaxed and I don't care what my mind thinks. Deep breaths as I sip the perfect blend of morning nectar, thinking that just maybe I could forget yesterday too, but I have this urge to apologize, a programmed response to make things right. I've screamed sorry, and it made no difference; I've also heard sorry so many times that it has no meaning; it's just something people say. Sorry must come with an action, not just a word response, so why am I saying sorry again? I pause in thought. This time I can't replay the scenario responses in my mind, and I can't run—where would I run to? If I hide, I could be lost, as I can't think of anyone who would even care.

My mind is my battlefield; many endless lost wars have played out there. It also can't be trusted. It's not like I'm some kind of mind reader. I wish I was, but I have learned to read people pretty well. One therapist explained that it's a survival tactic I developed to protect myself, but then alcohol plays the part of breaking that defence mechanism, which is why the only time I can avoid drinking is when I'm going through something. Being street smart really isn't smart at all.

I can do this; without wanting to hurt this gentle man any further, I must clean my side of the street without manipulation.

"Mathew, about yesterday, I just wanted to say I'm sorry, and I mean I'm sorry—"

He interrupts me. "Nichole, I'm sorry. I shouldn't have pushed you to face your emotions like I did. I know better, and I'm sorry."

I just got hit, like I have no idea how to respond to this. Stuttering to find the words to respond, thinking to myself that I can't not do this now, and besides, I will lose everything if I give up the money and the truth, I sit up confidently and reply, "I'm gonna take a bath and I borrowed some of Mum's clothes, if that's ok."

He smiles. "They're all yours. Relax, enjoy. I'm here for you, and, Nichole, I'm sorry also that I ignored your wishes to go back to your home. I just thought it best to rest first and see how you feel. Now, do you still want to go home? Because I can take you. We can stop all of this. I don't want to hurt you."

I'm completely thrown by his response, and my mind is silent but my body is tensing. I take a deep breath, and I'm remembering all the times I have been hurt before with nothing to gain. If I endure this pain, at least I get the money; what harm could possibly happen to me now? Even if he turns out to have manipulated me, I have more truth than I ever did before. Do I want to run and hide, or do I want to rise and fight? Then I hear an inner voice louder than the others. *Press through; I am with you.* Who is with me? This is not helping, but then it is, as it's calmer than the others, more reassuring and cheering me on instead of pulling me down—oh stop, mind, be still. I try to look Mathew in the eyes and respond with a shy but firm response.

"Mathew, it's ok. I will carry on, if only to see where this path leads. I'm gonna go for a bath first, and then see what the day unfolds. I can't promise anything, but I will try."

Mathew gives me a smile and says gently, "I got your back, Nichole. I won't allow anything or anyone harm you. I'm here just for you."

Ok, well, that is a response I've never had, so I'm going to choose to trust him and that's all I can do, however trust looks.

As I lie in the bath, I sink under the water. It's so quiet here: no voices, no noise, just peace, another way to calm. I feel a silence within, almost a happiness, not a care in the world, not a need to be met, just silence. I often think this must be how death feels. I'm not scared of death; I've fought him many times and won, sometimes barely hanging on, but I still won. So many have such a fear of death; I think if they had walked in my shoes, maybe they would lose that fear. Holding onto this life was never in my plan, but I dream of the next life being so much more deserving and freer; besides, ghosts can haunt and throw stuff around and scare the living, but then they can help the living too, I guess. Mindless thinking—ok, I'll get out, enough of this.

Have you ever wanted to be someone else, live in their shoes, wanting the freedom they take for granted? Trauma made me receive a life sentence of having so many voices, memories on constant replay, my brokenness. I never asked to be broken and unglued. There are so many things—from TV, music, smells, colours, even the way some people breathe—that can trigger me into a memory. I never get any good ones; they take me back when really I'm screaming forward. So many have said, "It's in your past, you need to get over it." No shit, Sherlock, but obviously I can't because it's a constant friend, a friend I never friended; it's like a ghost so it won't die. It never leaves me; it just lingers like sadness, regret, guilt, and shame.

Amazing, this dress fits perfectly, not tight at all. I love the long sleeves; I like the flow—ok, power face on, hair up, and I'm ready.

I want to sit in my place—it's safe—but I also want to go for a walk. I'll just sit and think about it; maybe Mathew has an exciting plan for today because yesterday was super boring and so draining. Over on the rocking chair is that red briefcase. Everything in me needs to know what's in it—it's mine after all—so I sit down and place it on the table and undo the two buckles. Looking inside, I notice it's full of papers, newspaper clippings, doctors' reports, and there's a red letter. It grabs my attention. It's from my dad. Strangely, excitement fills me.

My sweet baby girl,

I can only imagine the day you've had. If you're reading this, you didn't run away. I'm so proud of you for doing this journey with me. You're so strong and I admire you, just like your mum. Simon and Mark are great, aren't they? A lot to take in, I'm sure. It was for me also. Nichole, I spent far too many years in darkness, in anger because of these guys. I blamed them for it all. I believed they were my enemies, it was all their fault, but the truth is they suffered too. When I learned or, should I say, when I was ready to accept the truth, I was set free and so were they. I had to learn how to forgive, forgive them for the blame and pain I carried. I self-reflected like a mirror. I blamed them when the truth was, I blamed myself and carried all that guilt and shame around with me for too long.

It was a simple accident, not caused by them, by nature or even God. Finding blame for the pain was something I learned, so when I unlearned its power over me, I then had to learn how to forgive myself. Forgiving myself was when the true healing started to take place. I forgave myself for carrying all this pain, for choices I made, choices made from pain and trauma. I had to learn to fall in love with me and that I was worthy of such love. Losing your mum devastated me so much that I was now a victim trapped in a prison drowning in darkness. I couldn't even see or think of you and Andrew. I could only see what I had lost. I truly am so sorry, baby girl, my tinker bell. Oh, you were such a ball of energy, vibrant and always shining. I couldn't face you because then I would have to face myself.

I've arranged for today an adventure. Mathew has prepared and carried out all my plans for you to see the world as a different place. This is a dream I had that I wanted to do with your mum but never got the chance, but that's the thing with chances—when your open to them, seek them, you find that there's many more to be had. So today is your special day. Today is all about you. Just do one thing for me: I want you to really open your eyes and allow the beauty to feed *your heart. The world isn't a dark place, baby girl, when you feed your heart with beauty and love, the veil is removed and you will not only be able to see, feel, experience it, you'll also be able to receive it.*

I never stopped loving you and never will ❤

Forever your dad and you're forever my baby girl ❤

I feel like a little part of me just got healed, like truth hit my heart, like I'm more whole. Words are so powerful, especially when they're the ones you need to hear; even if they're written, they have the power to overwrite all the beliefs you've come to believe not only about yourself but life too. I'm not shaking; my mind is still in a state of deep thought, overwriting the lies I believed. My dad did love me, and I also understand him now too, actions I certainly would have probably done in his situation. I don't know if I'm ready to forgive that man Mark or myself, as I don't know how or why I should, but I learned this pain also and now I understand why Mathew said I needed to forgive myself. It's true—I am carrying my trauma around like an old dirty suit. It's heavy with years of dust settling on it, but how do I take it off? Is it really this easy? Oh my, there are so many people that hurt me; it would take forever to forgive them all, but wait, why should I? I never asked them to hurt me; I never asked them to take from me what wasn't theirs to take—my innocence. But wait, if healing is real, can it really be for me? Do I deserve it? I've made endless mistakes in my life, a lot of bad choices. Are they not mine to own? Do I not deserve these chains? Then a sweet soft voice interrupts my thinking: *You're looking at the effects of your trauma, not the cause. I love you.* I jolt back. Why do I have a voice inside me saying it loves me? Shaking my head, I wonder, Is this it? Am I really hearing this?

Can I be loved, am I worthy of love, do I even trust love? Yet inside I have craved it all my life but never found it, like I was running in circles and surrounded by broken glass, cutting my heels when I tried to find it. I have this deep yearning, so I know I don't think I ever truly gave up looking for it.

Mathew walks in. "Oh good, Nichole, you've read what the plan is for today. Here, have something to eat, and then after, we're going on an adventure. Have you ever been on a helicopter before?" He has this huge smile that could crack the earth in two.

"Mathew, can I ask you something please?"

He sits and replies, "Of course, Nichole."

Taking a deep breath, I say, "Mathew, is all of this real? Was it all truly planned for me, and why did he have to die for me to know him?"

As tears release from me, not just from my eyes but from deep within, Mathew takes a pause, comes closer to me. "I've known your dad since we were kids. He was the strongest out of us all; he stopped so many people from hurting us and took the pain himself. I personally owe him my life, so could I have imagined that he made the choice to leave you? No, Nichole, that truly did shock me. When your mum died, we all changed. For a time, we grew apart, not because we wanted to; none of us had prepared for the grief that happened. In our plan, we all grew old together and shared our war stories.

"When your dad was released from hospital, it devastated him to know we had already had the funeral. I remember taking him to her grave; he just stared and then I watched him turn dark. He left that night, and I didn't see or hear from him for many, many years. I tried to reach out a few times but got nothing. Then out of the blue, he shows up with Lesous. He was like a new man; it was like meeting him for the first time. All he wanted to do was talk. He talked about his journey through the pain, his darkness, and spoke so freely, like something I had never seen before. He had such a strength, such an energy that draws you in. He always did, but this was new.

"He spent the last three years planning this for you and Andrew. He wasn't stupid, he knew he couldn't just walk back into your life. He said his greatest regret was not being strong enough to go after you; it was a fear crippling him. He said the guilt of leaving you pushed him over the edge so many times, and he let her down by not coming for you. He said he didn't believe that he deserved to be happy without your mum. Oh, Nichole, how I want you to remember the love they had. I've never witnessed such love since, a love that was pure and unconditional, but then it did have a condition attached because when she died, so did he. I never knew him to manipulate anyone or any situation; his strength was truth, but then he walked in a powerful truth that would melt you just by witnessing.

"Nichole, this life is a wisp in the air, a droplet of rain. The experiences we have here truly do matter. Many walk around with a veil over them, which was placed over them through trauma, only seeing the personal outcome of their circumstances. Belief systems have taught them so many lies, that included me, until I learned how to walk again. I didn't lose my ability to physically walk, literally. I mean for the first time in my life, the mysteries of life were revealed to me, a new learning, a new life to be had. Anyways, Nichole, yes to your question. This is all very real, perfectly perfected for you, because you are their daughter and no situation could ever change that truth. You do matter, and one day, you will see what I see in you, so let's leave and see with anticipation what the day will reveal, Nichole. Even though you were not raised with them, you are like both of them; it's amazing to see, so come, let's go."

Again, as he smiles, I want to fall into him for a hug. His hug is so healing. Before I know it, I'm there again; his arm around me feels like the universe itself just held me. I'm shedding tears, but within, I feel like a little spark just ignited, a small spark of hope, of life.

"Yes, let's do this."

Chapter Eight

As we arrive at what appears to be a private airport, with maybe five hangers surrounded by big lights and a runway, there are people around who look like they're working, like mechanics but for planes. I feel so calm; my mind is excited. Are we going on a plane ride? Where will we go? Is it safe? What if we crash? Oh, mind, be still. Mathew asks me just to wait here as he goes to check to make sure everything's ready. He said we'll be going on a helicopter. I can feel such excitement. They look so cool in the movies. I've never been on one before; the closest I ever got was when I was in hospital, and when you heard the helicopter come in, you just knew it wasn't good for the passenger they were transporting, but in the movies I've seen, not the war ones, I'm taking about the ones where the people escape—I always wanted to be that person who could escape in one. They kinda look like dragonflies—I love dragonflies. I feel like I'm a little girl, excitement, anticipation, and curiosity flooding through my mind and body. Where are we going?

I can see Mathew next to a blood-red helicopter. He's talking to the driver; the driver is a woman. I didn't know there were women drivers—amazing. I can just see her flowing blond hair as she ties it up in a bun. She's smiling at Mathew in her uniform, which is blood red with a black belt around her tiny frame. She puts her helmet on, and that's when Mathew starts walking back towards me—oh, I feel so excited. He goes into the back seat, pulling out three black bags. I didn't even notice they were there.

"Nichole, you ready?" He smiles, of course. I'm ready. I'm shaking from the excitement; I think my cheeks are going to hurt from smiling: "Yes, Yes I'm ready." As we walk across the field, I look over to the hangers and notice everyone is standing and staring at us, just smiling—that's weird.

"Mathew, what is this place?"

"Oh sorry, Nichole. This is your dad's. I guess now it's yours and Andrew's. I'll explain more later."

All of a sudden, I feel rich—never in my wildest dreams could I have imagined this. Did my dad fly planes? Can I learn? Oh, I'm so excited. As the helicopter starts, its engine and those huge blades start to spin—which, by the way, look so much bigger the closer you get—we get into our seats in the back, and Mathew asks if he can help buckle me in. "Of course, please help," I chuckle. My helmet is on; Mathew tells me that we have to talk through the mouthpieces and built-in headphones. Oh, I'm so excited. As he gets himself prepared, I can now hear his voice in my head—that's too funny. He gives me a thumbs up, taps the driver's shoulder, and we're ready. There's a feeling of being in a lift, where your stomach tries to reach back for the ground, and we're up—wow, it's fast.

Mathew is smiling as he speaks. "Nichole, first we are going to fly over your hometown. I want you to see everything from this view. Trust me, it will give you a different perspective, as everything will be smaller and have a different meaning."

Whatever does he mean? As I gaze out of the window, I see houses approaching. They look so small; the trees too. I can't see any people; everything looks like squares. It looks amazing, so beautiful. Mathew points down. "That's your house right there."

Inside Me

I can barely see it; we're just circling around a small place. Oh my, from here, you can also see the old bridge, which looks more like a log over a stream, not as threatening. We're getting higher; now we're going over trees, gliding over them. The mountains look much closer, and this is fun. I am completely blown away by all the beauty; we're going through the clouds, clouds I always imagined I could bounce around on as I jump from the mountain tops. As we glide over a mountain like the wind is leading us, I see a lake— it's amazing, a lake so high up. Mathew grabs my hand. "Nichole, we're here."

I'm focused now on the surroundings. The trees start to look bigger as we go down. There's a field we're aiming for; I can't for the life of me imagine what could possibly be the reason for being here, but I'm so excited. Even if it was just the ride, I'll be so happy. As we hit the ground, I can see a house with someone standing in front, on the porch. I tug at Mathew.

"Look, there's someone here."

Mathew smiles. "Of course, Nichole, let's go meet him; he's been expecting you."

I don't know if it's adrenaline pumping through me, but I feel excited. We unbuckle, and Mathew grabs our bags. It's so windy I have an automatic response to bend as I walk under those propellers, thinking they could certainly take my head off. Could you imagine after all this that that's what takes me out? Ha ha.

I look over at the lake; with the sun shining, it looks like a million diamonds glistening. At the side of the house, there's a huge tree. I've never seen one so big in width before; it must be thousands of years old; it's amazing. I can see under it that there's a wooden bench and a little table with a vase of what looks like wildflowers. I can see lavender and daisies, I think; it's so beautiful. I can hear so many singing birds. Oh look, there's a mother duck with a blanket of yellow babies following her—how adorable.

It's breathtaking. The house is an old log cabin, big, with many windows and three levels. Fruit trees to the right of it—wait, it's too early for ripe fruit, yet I see red apples; they look ready to eat, so many of them. The porch looks like it wraps around the house. The wood is dark and oily, making it shine as the sun's rays hit it. There are so many flowers of every kind and colour, and then I notice the lilies, so many of them; this place really is heaven on earth—so amazing—the air is filled with a fresh fragrance and it's so clean.

I can hear the birds more clearly now as the helicopter leaves in the distance; then I see him—a man coming down the three steps of the porch, towards us. He's so tall, wearing all white; he has curly golden-blond hair; his skin is tanned like he's from the Middle East—it's healthy, like he glows; perfect lips with the most amazing white teeth; his smile feels like it could heal the world. Oh, his eyes—as he gets closer, his eyes make me want to turn away. They are a striking blue that I can't describe; I feel so drawn in like his whole being is a magnet. Who is this man?

"Mathew, Nichole, welcome. I have been waiting for you with great anticipation. How was your journey?"

Mathew goes in to give him a hug, like they're brothers. Oh, I do hope I don't have to hug, as he draws his attention now towards me. "Don't worry, Nichole. You're safe here, and I won't make you hug me."

Did he really just say that? Can he read minds? His eyes—it feels like he's reading my soul; there's such a warmth about him. I honestly cannot describe it, as I have nothing to compare it to, not anything I've ever seen before. As we follow him towards the house, I feel like I'm floating. My body is calm, almost like marshmallows, if that even makes any sense. My mind is racing, though, racing like it has all come to the surface, not its usual arguments but full of intrigue and questions. Who is he?

Then he turns to me and smiles. "Nichole, I'm Lesous, in case you're wondering." Well, that didn't relax my mind; now there are more questions, but wait—it's not the end; I'm supposed to meet him at the end. He turns to me again. "Don't worry, Nichole, not only do I have all the answers to your questions, but I also have the solutions too."

His smile, his words are so soothing. He really can read my mind. What kind of guru is he? He bursts out laughing; he turns to Mathew.

"Mathew, you know where to take the bags, and I'll take Nichole to the sunroom. We'll wait for you there." As we walk through the house, a sweet fragrance fills the air. There's so much light in here; you'd assume it would be dark, hidden under the trees. In front of a rock-walled fireplace in which logs burn is a red sofa with huge arms. It looks like you could fall into it; it looks so comfy. There's a sheepskin rug laid on the wooden floor, with huge vases filled with lilies on each side. Above the fire on the mantle, there are three old candles. I say old because they're so big they could burn forever. Behind the sofa is a table with a brass lamp like the one in my mum's house. There are so many pictures on the walls—oh wait, they're all of children: some in fields of flowers, laughing, some splashing under waterfalls, some climbing trees. I love this room; it's so relaxing and peaceful.

As Lesous walks through, ushering me with an under wave of his hand, I follow him under a huge archway, passing the kitchen, which I only get a quick glance of. Then he goes through a glass door, which looks made of crystal as it's filled with rainbows as the light hits it. I continue following him through. I can feel what I can only describe as a deep inner peace. The room is made of glass, or crystal, I'm not sure; it's so bright—oh, this must be the sunroom. I can see why he called it that, as it's filled with so much light. There are three red chairs—they must match the sofa, as they too look like you could fall into them; a little table in between them with a vase of lilies; the coffee table has a jug of what looks like lemon water with three glasses and another large candle lit; there's a sheep rug under it too. The floor also looks like it's made of coloured glass; even though this room is filled with light, it's not blinding. Why do I feel so unworthy to be here? This place makes me feel so dirty and poor; this isn't for people like me.

He asks me to sit next to him as he pats the chair. My body feels like it's crying as I drag it over to sit. It's only bones and skin with a few organs inside to keep it functioning; my mind controls it, making every movement like it is not a part of me. As I fall into the chair, I'm thankful the back cushion will keep me forward as I stare down at my bones for legs; why can't I look up? I have never felt this way before; I don't feel attacked or the need to run; I don't feel like I'm being punished or about to have to give my body to him. None of the feelings I normally get around a man when I'm feeling so vulnerable are there; what is this? As he takes a deep breath with his eyes closed, I can't stop looking at his face. It's so perfect—not a spot, scar, or blemish—then he opens his eyes, looks straight into mine, and I'm listening, waiting in anticipation for him to speak. He smiles and then, "Nichole, you have come so far in your life, and with this journey, you needed help. You need to know that nothing you've gone through was your fault. You are right; you never asked for any of it. I knew today you needed truth and healing."

I interrupt. "Why? Do I have cancer? Do you know that?"

"No, Nichole, you don't have cancer. Your soul needs healing; your body needs healing. Let me explain. Here, have a drink of water; it will replenish you."

Oh, how I wish this water was wine. I could really use a drink. Then, as I take a sip, oh my god—it tastes like wine. I look and it is wine. "What magic is this?" I jolt back in my seat, looking at the red liquid where the water was. Am I losing my mind finally? He looks at me, laughing.

"It's not magic; it's not trickery at all. Turning water into wine is easy for me. I just knew what you needed."

Confused, I respond, "What do you mean? Can you really read my mind?"

Now he's looking serious. "Nichole, it's not about reading your mind. Your mind is your soul, and I know your soul so very well. Giving you wine is a body's need response to escape. I don't want you to feel you need to escape; I want you to be in the moment, this moment. It won't get you drunk, but it will help your body to relax."

As I take another sip, it's so sweet but not like pop or juice, nothing like I've ever tasted before—must be what the rich people drink, not the box wine I'm used to. "Here, Nichole, have some bread. It will help to absorb the wine. A little wine is good for your stomach." Where did the bread come from? I love bread; it's definitely a comfort food for me. I bite into it, pulling back. It's so chewy and the smell of yeast isn't there, but the taste is almost sweet. As I breathe it in, I can feel my body relax and the only thoughts going through my mind are, How can I keep him? Weird, but that's all I'm thinking.

Mathew enters the room and sits down; he's smiling, of course, as he looks over at me and then speaks to this man. "Lesous, is there anything you need me to do?"

"My dear Mathew, just having you present is all I need you to be. Nichole has comfort in you, so that's all that's required." They exchange smiles. As I'm chugging down the bread and amazing wine, I'm feeling only what I could call special. I have done nothing to deserve this, and I also don't know what to do with it. I feel like a child, a little girl, waiting for the adults to direct me. I don't know why I'm not wanting to run right now, but I feel safe, which is extremely odd. It's almost like I need a reboot, reprogramming; everything I ever learned is all jumbled, and confusing flashes of memories, which I used to suppress, are now at the surface. But I don't have the body responses like I normally do. I feel so relaxed, like I'm looking at someone else's story, their life so distant from my own. Receiving visions and watching the sexual abuse, I see a little girl crying after but so tense and unaware whilst it's happening; the mere thought of this would trigger me and cause my body to lock down, searching for something to escape to. Oh, my poor liver—I started drinking at ten, not often back then, but I remember my body was so relaxed. The bruises I had were rarely on the outside; they were bursting on the inside, like millions of cells turning into tumours waiting to explode. I'm watching all the people screaming at her, rejecting her, and not caring for her needs. I burst out, "She's just a little girl. Someone needs to stop this!"

Lesous grabs my hand. "Nichole, that little girl is you, and yes, she does need protecting, not violating. Can you see every time she tries to cry out, the people around her think she's angry and punish her for it, when the truth is what happened to her is not lost or forgotten? It does matter, and she was not in control of any of it. It wasn't her fault, Nichole. It wasn't your fault and you did nothing wrong to deserve this."

I interrupt. "Then why did it happen? Why did it happen to me? If not my fault, then whose?"

Lesous takes a breath and then says, "Nichole, let me show you what I know. Let me show you the truth." As he says that, I get a flood of visions: I see adults beating their children; children left alone in rooms crying; men and women going into their rooms whilst they're asleep, violating them or beating them; adults drinking and passing out whilst their children are looking for food; children crying for their parents, searching for them. I see them asking strangers if they know where their parents are. I see an old lady beating them with a cane as the children are hiding under the table. I see wars; there are soldiers searching through houses, stealing all the possessions and raping women and children.

"Ok enough. This is too much to see. Who are these people?"

Lesous looks like he's so sad. "Nichole, these are the people that hurt you—it's their lives, their parents. A child has so few needs, but when the parents are full of trauma and stress, they can't see the needs of their child. Some will even try to buy their child everything it wants but fail to give them the one thing they need more than material items; they need to know they're loved. They need the time of the parent and to see the parent laugh with them and love them, teach them to see the world instead of making the world feel it's not a safe place to be, or that their bodies are not a safe place to be in. When the parent is always stressed, the child feels this and feels unsafe and rejected, so what is the child to do but to try to please the parent? The child can take on the role, believing it's their responsibility to make the parent happy, when the truth is, it's the child's role to learn healthy love, to learn how to see the world in its true beauty, and most importantly, the child needs to be heard, know its voice matters, know its life matters."

I go off into thought. Am I supposed to feel sorry for them, that they made my life a living hell because of their own? What am I supposed to do with this? Normally, anger rages inside me at the mere thought that they did this to me and especially because they should have known better if this happened to them. They should have known how it felt, but the anger is not there. My body is relaxed in response. Then, I hear a faint voice inside, *Forgive them.* You are kidding me, seriously.

Lesous interrupts. "Let me explain forgiveness. To forgive also means to give up. When you give up something, it's because you no longer want it, to keep it means you're attached to it, like a noose around your neck always pulling you down. When you forgive, you give yourself the honour you deserve to not carry it anymore. Holding on keeps you in bondage with the person and persons that hurt you.

"When you look at yourself as a three-part being, you are made into body, soul, and spirit. The bondage traps your being into different parts so it's impossible to be whole, and the memory is always there at the surface no matter what you do to escape or try to drown it out, so the power used to harm you isn't released; to release it is to forgive. It doesn't mean you forget or no longer hold that person or persons accountable; it means you've given them up to a greater power than yourself. There is always accountability for causing someone trauma. It's never forgotten. It does matter. You matter and your voice does get heard. Your body will create a false armour around itself, wanting to protect; your soul will constantly be reminding you of the pain and want justice.

"When you forgive, you no longer judge, a power you can do nothing with. Hand it all over, hand it to me; give me all the burdens of your heart. I will take them away and then you will be free and no longer attached to them, and that's when the real healing starts."

Why do I feel so calm, like there's a blanket around me?

"How do you take it all away? There's so much."

He looks serious, with what I can only describe as compassion. "Just wanting to and saying out loud 'I forgive them,' I can work with that; I can move in your life with just you wanting to be free, releasing them all to me. Try it and I'll show you."

I really want to be free. For the first time in my life, I can see a future and I want to let go of the past. It's not helping me; it's isolating me. "Ok, I will try but don't leave me." Then within a second, the memories come flooding in as I feel him holding my hand. He, too, is in the memories. I can see him holding me after each violation; I can see him crying with me; I can see him standing in front of people, taking the punches for me. As I say to each one, "I forgive you," I can see them disappear like a wisp of dark smoke, vanishing, and my body jolts each time as if I'm releasing something, tears pulling from my body, crying in places I didn't know I could cry.

Then I see my daughter—a deep emptiness comes over me. I see him standing over her, he's saying, "Release her by forgiving yourself. You did not kill her; she died in her sleep, and she's with me." I say the words and I see her surrounded by what I can only describe as angels, taking her from the crib, awakening her from her sleep. She is smiling and so full of colour, not like the darkness of death I have in my mind; she looks at me and says, "I love you, Mummy. I'm safe now." As she smiles, I feel like my head is going to explode with pressure, and she's talking. She was only babbling at four months. How can this be? My entire body is shaking, yearning to hold her one last time, and that's when the angels bring her over and place her next to my chest. I can feel her, she's warm, and she's mine again. She says, "Forgive yourself, Mummy. You need to let me go. I'll visit you on all your happy days. As I grow, I will not forget you."

As soon as she says this, I let her go, not because I wanted to but because she wanted to. She looks so happy and free; I didn't know I had trapped her to me. My entire being cries out the years of pain. I was only seventeen when I had her and eighteen when she died, and no one could tell me why. She was the first person to love me unconditionally. As I breathe deep, I can feel something releasing me, something leaving; my body relaxes; a peace washes over me in waves. I feel clarity in my mind. The fountains of tears flowing start to cease like I've cried my last cry, and now I feel like I know where she is. I got to see her one more time, to hold her, and she knows I love her, and I feel forgiven.

As I open my eyes, he reaches over and rubs my cheeks. I see him take my tear on his finger, rubbing it into his cheek. I feel like I'm connecting to him. I can barely describe this feeling; it's like nothing I've ever had before, but if this is how love feels, then I'm feeling it.

Chapter Nine

When my daughter died, I lost the biggest part of me, a part I had no intention or desire to find. I was ok in my grief; I felt I deserved this pain; I was surviving through life anyways. I had no one to talk to about it because I didn't know how to cope with keeping the wound open, doing everything I could to drown out the pain. But what I do know is that no one wanted to talk about it because they couldn't fix me, so I pushed it down, pushed so far down that I no longer had it, at least that's what I believed.

Now all I can see is her in beauty, instead of the darkness of death imprinted in my mind. When your heart breaks the way mine did, it's not an easy fix, and saying "Just get over it and on with your life" is the worst thing you can ever tell anyone. Obviously, I couldn't because it was lingering in the back of my mind, in my quiet thoughts, torturing me; then when I did talk about it to professionals, I realized that all I was doing was venting, but it never fixed anything; it just helped me to compartmentalize my thoughts, fears, and emotions, to put them back in neat filing cabinets. All the while, I was punishing myself and my body; my body was never a safe place to be in; the world surrounding me was not a safe place. I was merely existing, and I was almost a pro at making it look like I had it altogether, until I was alone with my own memories, a life I didn't choose, pleading for my traumas to be someone else's dramas. I wasn't angry at the world or angry at God; I was angry with myself, filled with shame and guilt, believing it was all my fault, that if I had been better behaved, then none of the terrible things would have happened to me. But it was all a lie, and that's what I learned. I had to learn with my eyes open to the truth that everyone is not immune from trauma and pain, that everyone goes through something in life, and then I had to learn that the world is a beautiful place, that I can see beauty in everything, even the weeds, that I don't have to look for it, I'm actually surrounded by it.

My pain hid me from seeing this; it hid me and wanted me to suffer more, so the lessons I've learned, which have set me free, led me on a journey of self-discovery: Who am I? Why am I here? Instead of, Why was I even born? I had to learn love. I had been taught that love can be taken away, that I wasn't worthy of it, that it had conditions always attached, that it was only sexual and not comforting, that it was based only on a reward for performance. I had to learn that true love is not a feeling or a reward, that true love is unconditional regardless of what you do or don't do. It isn't earned; it's all about growing in a relationship without expectations; it's full of trust, grace, and acceptance. I had to learn to love me because I am worthy to be loved.

As I lie back in the chair, floods and waves of peace flow over me, unlocking the chains that had me bound, and I realize that this must be how freedom feels, for me anyways. I don't want to open my eyes; I don't want this to ever end. I want to stay in this moment forever; in this moment, I finally feel free.

I can feel the rays of sun on my face. I can hear the trees blowing in the wind, birds singing in sync a most beautiful song. I can smell the flowers faint in the air. I can feel my body, almost like it's talking to me, telling me that it missed me. For years, I had not wanted this body; I blamed this body; this body was the reason

I was so violated and made my world not safe. I remember a time when I left my body and stood over it, watching the pain as if it was happening to someone else. I didn't know it was a part of me. I didn't know I couldn't come back; I thought I was stuck in it. Then Lesous says in such a soft voice, "Nichole, your body isn't ugly and worn out—it's beautiful: each limb working to help you day to day; your organs perfectly functioning to break down the nutrients and your digestive system assisting you to remove dangerous toxins and waste; your heart beating, pushing blood throughout your system every second. Your heart was never broken, not in the physical sense, but in the spiritual one; your heart is the realm where all your broken pieces are. Many are whole now and healed. It's a beautiful place made to protect you. You see, if this place didn't exist, then neither would you. You were never created to take on that much pain and trauma, so it was created to protect you, each piece holding onto the memories and rising up to take pain because you couldn't anymore; and now is the time to heal."

As I'm listening, I have no idea what he's on about. My understanding of the body is at a minimum level; I was never that interested. Actually, not true—I was interested when I thought I destroyed my kidneys and liver. I got so paranoid that I had to try to fix it. I shudder at the memory of those horse pills, yuk. There were times in my life, I cared about my body, but only when I thought I would die. I feared death more than I did life, if I'm completely honest, but that realization only came when my body was breaking down. My body was the only thing I could control. I controlled what I ate; starving myself did give me a deep feeling of some control, but then I got cravings and, in my mind, when I looked in the mirror, I looked like a whale, but then the moment I threw it up, I felt like I'd got my figure back. Remembering the scar tissue in my throat and the doctor's comments, I wonder if any part of my body isn't scarred or damaged. I'm really not feeling too good right now; I want that euphoric feeling back. I was sur-rounded by magic mirrors my whole life, but not the ones that tell you how amazingly beautiful you are; mine always reminded me of the things that needed improving; every scar was magnified in this mirror. I've broken so many mirrors; maybe that's why I had so much bad luck.

Lesous interrupts, "Nichole, there's no such thing as luck; breaking mirrors or not breaking them does not define your future; it just gives many a reason for their past. Everyone is searching for some kind of meaning to their past. The truth is, your past can either destroy you or refine you, but it should never define who you are. In this world, there is always beauty hidden and many find it. You found it in the most peculiar places—you're finding it now. When we stop searching for these meanings as to why and start searching for healing, we break the life mirror. We stop searching for answers that can never be humanly answered.

"Every war that was created by man was always blamed by reli-gion; every time a child dies, this is blamed on an unloving god who would give the gift of life and then take it away again, leaving the person or persons feeling like there's an answer. No one is immune here from pain; death does come to all here, but eternal life—now that does have a decision; people do get to decide how that is spent."

I'm feeling angry as I interrupt, "Oh great, so you're now going to remind me I'm going to hell. Great, just what I need. Someone already beat you to that punchline, yet the person didn't even know me or know that I was already in hell. How dare you bring that up?"

He interrupts, "Oh, Nichole, people have used that excuse for centuries. They read the book, and all of sudden, they believe they know the meaning and mysteries of the world, using it to control the lost and wounded, and trying in their own words and works to be the voice of God, believing they're doing right. But the most important part of it all is they forget the love, which is mentioned over five hundred times in the Bible. There is no excuse to why they do this, but it never goes unnoticed; it's always noted and remembered. But instead of me trying to explain, come with me, let me show you some examples."

I really don't care to know what he's going on about. I'm remembering this one family I was with, they preached to me day and night. They said I was full of demons and that God was punishing me, but it was because He loved me. Dragging me off to their church where they had all their cliques of friends, yet I would hear them judging those that didn't belong to their group. No thanks, I want nothing to do with them, spending eternity with them—definitely no thanks. I'm intrigued, though, to see what he wants to show me.

"Fine, show me."

No sooner have I said that when I leave my body, floating through the air or time. . . . I say this because it's like a million colours surrounding me; I see nothing, just colours. Then within seconds, we are in a place. I look over and there are people shouting and they sound angry. We walk through the crowd. I think we are invisible because no one is looking at us; we actually walk through them like ghosts. Then at the front of the crowd, we see a huge bonfire. Oh my, there's a woman tied to it. It looks like they're going to burn her.

"What is this? Someone, stop this!"

The people are dressed like they're in the past, like really in the past. The people are holding lanterns and sticks with fire. This must be one of those re-enactments but, wait, I flew here. I tug at Lesous. "What is this?" He's crying, tears are flooding down his cheeks, he says, "See, Nichole, just listen to what they're saying."

As I tune in, they're all chanting, "Kill her, kill the witch." Others, "The devil's whore, kill her." They're all so angry; then someone who looks like a monk starts to speak. "You have been found guilty in the eyes of God for witchcraft and sentenced to death by the flames of God and may God have mercy upon your soul." Then he lights the flames and the crowd cheers and laughs. I can't see the woman's face—it's hidden with a mask—but I know it's a woman because of her figure.

"Lesous, stop this. How can we stop this?" I start screaming for them to stop but nothing—no one is listening. They're all just laughing; then I see what looks like angels take her ghost as the flames start to touch her feet. She looks amazing. I hear her like a loud speaker say, "Forgive them, for they do not know what they do. Don't hold this debt against them." She then smiles and is taken up; it is beautiful. Then I turn and ask him what the meaning of all this is, as he's now smiling straight at her as she looks back and smiles at him. He says, "Nichole, her names Angelina, and as a small girl, she had such a love to see people healed and happy. As she grew, she discovered the healing properties in plants and healed and cared for many. There was a man who was offering money to the poor if they gave up all the witches in the land, and this man gave her up as he had a family to feed. She wasn't a witch; she was my child, and I knew her very well."

As he's telling me this, I can see everything he's describing; I can feel her pain and how they did this in the name of God. He responds, "Yes, Nichole, God gets blamed for so much, yet He had nothing to do with it."

Just then, we're flying again, all the amazing colours swirling around us like northern lights, which I have only seen on TV, so I'm really enjoying the colours. I can't describe it and how my body is completely relaxed; my mind is still yet I feel an excitement, even though I just witnessed something so cruel and unjust. Then we hit the ground. Now we're at another angry mob of people, and we appears to be in the present. They seem to be protesting outside a building; they're holding placards which read, *Forgiveness for the sin of abortion; God is watching you. Abortion is murder; Repent and turn from your sins; Murder is a ticket to hell.* I can hear someone talking on a loud speaker; he says that judgement from God is going to fall on this place of hell.

"Oh, Lesous, what is this place? Where are we?"

He says nothing, but he looks angry. Then suddenly, we're inside a building. I see women hugging crying women; it's a waiting room; young girls and older ones, too, are sitting in hospital gowns; they look like they're so broken, staring at the ground with the world on their shoulders. Then I hear a girl's name being called. We follow her in. They ask her to lie on the bed and explain the doctor will be here soon as a nurse lays a blanket over her legs, then puts her feet in stirrups and tells her to bend her knees and bring her bum forward. The girl turns away and cries. I see Lesous reach for her hand; can she see us? The nurse soothes her with kind words, telling her she'll be ok, this will be over soon. Then the doctor comes in and another person; he sits on a stool at the end of her bed, between her legs. The other one stands at her head, putting a mask over her face, whispering, "This will help. You'll fall asleep and when you awake, it will all be over." She's still crying. I look to Lesous; he is also crying. As she counts back from ten, she goes to sleep, and the nurse hands the doctor something that looks like a metal stick with tubing attached. I look to see where he's going with that as he lifts the blanket and enters it into her womb. Just then the room is filled with those angels again; I see them reach inside her womb also and, oh my, they have a baby— it's so tiny. They're smiling as they look at Lesous; then the ceiling opens, I can see what looks like a ladder and the angels go with the baby and climb the ladder; then I hear a machine go on. The clear tube is now red; the liquid is filling up what looks like a blender.

He's looking at a screen then he says, "I think I got it all," which makes me realize in shame that I know exactly what's going on. I'd completely blocked this memory from my mind—that girl is me, over twenty years ago now. As soon as the memory floods in, I can feel a gut-wrenching pain in my stomach; it's like my body remembers. I'm trying to search for excuses. "Lesous, I was so young. I couldn't have a baby. I was a baby myself and homeless. I had no support, no one to help me. The father was abusive; he would have killed me. I couldn't . . ."

Just then Lesous interrupts me with his eyes filled with tears, and speaks in a low, soothing voice as he holds my cheeks. "Nichole, you were not alone, and I knew this day would come. You need to forgive yourself; you've carried this guilt and shame around with you for too long. Your daughter did not die because you did this; God is not punishing you; you have punished yourself. You believed those people outside the clinic, believing they were representatives of God. They were not. They judged you, and they will be held accountable for their actions."

Then he grabs my hand and leads me up the ladders in the sky. We climb and climb, and it feels like we're walking on clouds; then in the distance, I see an opening. I can see butterflies at the entrance, so many of them strangely bright coloured, just so beautiful; then I see a stream, and as I look in the water, I can see children playing and splashing. On the field next to it, a field filled with flowers like a huge blanket, I see children running and laughing. In the trees, the children are playing on swings, and there are angels playing with them. In the air is a sweet fragrance, like actual sweets. The calmness here I cannot describe; the colours I also cannot describe.

Lesous is so happy here. As he waves his hand, I can see a few little children run towards us, skipping and smiling. There are two little boys and two little girls of different ages. As they come closer, I notice one little girl looks like me when I was that age, except she is happy; her hair is like mine: it's long, past her hips, curly and a golden red, exactly like mine. She's wearing a beige floral dress with little white ankle socks and beige ballet shoes. Her eyes are dark brown like mine, almost black like mine. The oldest one is a boy. He looks so familiar. He has tight curls of brown hair, and dark brown eyes. His build is strong set. He's wearing a light blue short-sleeved shirt and beige pants. The other boy is much younger. He has wavy, shoulder-length red hair, green eyes, and lots of freckles around his nose. He's more of a skinny build, and he's wearing a white T-shirt with blue jeans. The youngest little girl has beautiful blond locks, more like golden—it's long, thick, and curly. Her eyes are so blue, and her complexion is pure white. She's wearing a lilac-coloured dress with tiny white flowers, and her socks match with black little ballet shoes.

Oh, they all have the button nose like me. I'm almost too scared to ask, and then Lesous interrupts, thankfully. "Nichole, these are your children. They have been so excited waiting for today. All line up—eldest first. This is Michael, Antony, Justyce, and Simone. They have a song prepared for you." I see them all smiling and all I can feel is my heart break; I can't hold the tears back. "I am so sorry; I didn't know. I believed you were not babies yet; I didn't know and how did you get your names? I never named you."

The eldest little boy comes forward, and they're all crying. "Mummy, don't cry. We don't hold this against you. We love coming to visit you on all your happy days. We're happy."

I look at Lesous. "I didn't know; I'm so sorry."

He holds me and whispers in my ear, "Nichole, you're forgiven, as I knew everything before it was ever done, and I also knew this day would come. Everything's perfectly planned out. Forgive yourself; you must to be free."

My cheeks flow with tears, down my neck like a waterfall. I take a deep breath; then in my mind, I say I forgive myself. As soon as I do, I feel something release me and something enter, which I can only describe as a feeling that I'm more complete, if that makes any sense. Then I open my eyes, and we're in a stadium. There's a baby grand piano on a stage, and the girl playing—it is amazing; the sound is perfect, not that I know much about how pianos play; I just love the sound. She has thick long curly red hair and a petite little body. As they all are standing around the piano, Lesous whispers, "The girl playing is your daughter Maxie. She is so much like you, strong willed, very bright, full of wisdom, always walking with such a grace about her. She's been preparing all this for you, even the special guest." He's smiling so much as I'm crying so much; even though my heart should be breaking, I feel like it's becoming whole again. It's the weirdest feeling.

I try to take in this moment with as many memories of details as I can. I never want this to end; I don't want to leave this place. She is so beautiful. Just then—oh my, is that really him? Lesous nods a yes and smiles. It's Michael Jackson. He comes on the stage dancing and smiling, and then he's singing a song that I love, "Man in the Mirror," as the stage lights up and butterflies fill the atmosphere. Michael, Antony, Justyce, and Simone are dancing so amazingly beautiful, along with Michael Jackson. My heart is filled with what I can only describe as a feeling that my skin will burst with excitement, joy, and such a great peace. I don't even feel like I want to escape, like I need to run or drown out; I am fully present in the moment, in this moment, and this moment is mine.

They all take a bow and fireworks light up the sky. They're all laughing and giggling, and then Maxie walks over to me. My entire body crumbles to the floor. She's not a baby anymore; she's a beautiful young lady, so beautiful as the light hits her hair, shining in many colours, smiling with her perfect smile. She holds out her hand to lift me up. I can't—I feel like I'm stuck to floor. "Mummy, you are so beautiful. I have missed you so much since I last saw you, which was actually last week, ha ha. Thank you for loving me because your love brought desires into my heart to fulfil dreams. I teach ballet here and get to rub shoulders with some pretty amazing artists."

Lesous touches my hand, and I feel like I'm filling up with a warm fluid, but not fluid—oh, I can't describe it—but it gives me the power to stand and hold my daughter again as an adult. But how has she grown? I just held her as a baby. Then Lesous whispers, "Time is for where you are. A thousand years here is a day to you there; nobody ages here unless they want to. There is no sickness or disease because there is no death. This is an eternal resting place and here you are free from all pain."

As I listen with my heart, I say to Lesous, "I want to stay here; I want to stay forever. Can I, please?" He smiles, grabs my hand. I look over and see my children smiling and waving at me, and then I fall asleep in such peace. My heart is at rest.

Chapter Ten

As I awake from the most amazing weird dream, I stretch out my arms and open my eyes.

"Where am I?"

This room is not familiar. It doesn't look like anyone is next to me. There are so many pillows, and they're so soft. I'm in a four-poster bed with red velvet curtains closing it in like a box. The posts have the most amazing carvings—oh my—and the blanket is heavy. I feel like I'm being held. Wait, I can hear voices in the distant; people are laughing but not a sarcastic laugh, genuine laughter. It's like an old movie set. I pull back the curtain on my right, and there's a huge multi-coloured stained glass window with so much light shining through but not blinding, and red velvet drapes over the edge of the dark, carved wooden frame and a huge red chair in the corner with a golden cushion. The table next to it, in front of the window, is covered in wildflowers in crystal vases and so many candles. The fragrance is so sweet. This room is like heaven, but where am I?

Just then the door opens and a soft sweet lady's voice says, "Hello, Nichole, my name is Gwenlynn. May I come in? How was your rest?"

A young woman enters. She's so beautiful with locks of cara-mel-coloured hair floating down her face, a golden completion with the whites of her eyes so wide and shining like light, bringing out her hazel circles with flecks of green. She smiles, and her teeth are perfect with a centre gap on top. Her lips are full and have a natural red to them. She's beautiful; what must she think of me? I'm all bony and worn out, full of scars on the outside and even more on the inside. Why is she so nice to me? Wait, who is she and where am I? I sit up promptly at the end of the bed. Looking down, I have a white nightie on, like one of those from the really old movies with lace edgings. My little feet peeping out have traces of old pink nail varnish on my ugly toe nails.

She places some clothes over the chair, and in a beautiful soft voice, says, "Here, Nichole, I hope you like what I chose for you to wear, and I would love to do your hair for you."

As she reaches over to remove some random pieces of my hair floating over my eyes, I jolt back as I feel violated. She smiles. "I'll wait for you in the living room. Lesous is there, and we will explain everything."

I feel an excitement. I feel a familiar feeling also of loss and not knowing where I am, but it is also comforting because in the past week, it's been so exciting. As I rise from the bed to see what clothes are there, I get a peek outside. Oh my, the garden with many flowers and trees. There's a golden path glistening around it like a maze of some sort, and a water fountain with huge streams of water, which almost reach up to my window. It's so beautiful. I reach for the clothes and feel intriguing excitement. The shirt is long; it's cream and it's plain, which is good. The pants are a deep purple, not a colour I've ventured before, but it will work, and underwear. Oh good, there's a basin of water with steam rising out, a bar of soap, and a really, I mean really, soft towel. As I start to wash, it's almost like I can feel the years falling off my face as the water is absorbed into every pore. The soap is more like a cream with a faint fragrance of jasmine. Within seconds, I'm dressed and ready, but it felt like hours. As I open my eyes, the room is clean, the bed is made, the curtains around it are open and tied back, yet I didn't know anyone was in here except me.

No sooner do I wonder where I am to go than I'm there, transported into the very room, sitting on a huge comfy cream chair, which feels like one big cushion. I don't know how I got here. Lesous is sitting across from me on a cushion on the floor in front of a carved oak table, and on the table is a china tea set. It's white with gold trim. The lady Gwenlynn is pouring tea into three cups. They look so happy. The room is large but cozy, filled with antique furnishings, from Welsh dressers full of more china, to cabinets topped with many gold-framed photos. The frame around the fireplace is carved wood, as well as the frame around the three windows, which are also coloured paned glass. The floor is white carpet with little red roses in pattern, matching the wallpaper. There are flowers in many vases and ones that I have not seen before, but they're beautiful and some a little weird but in a unique way. The room's fragrance is like roses but also peaches.

I cannot describe how I feel in this room as I've never felt this way. I feel so relaxed, my body is in a state of shock, I think, and it's not in its usual needy self. I have no desire to run, to try to leave it behind, or exhaust it into rest—I just can't describe it. It's taking all the courage I have to ask, "Where am I and how did I get here?"

They both lock eyes and, smiling, Lesous turns to me. "Nichole, let me introduce to you your great-great-grandmother. She's been waiting for you with great anticipation, and we're here to show you truth so you can be free."

Ok, that woke me up—seriously, my great-great-grandmother, seriously? Now I'm more confused than ever but also have a deep sense of wanting this to be true. I respond in a sheepish, puzzled voice, "How can this be? She's so young."

As she sits down beside me on the edge of the chair, she laughs, not a mocking laugh but a cute one. "Oh, my dear, thank you, that's quite the compliment. I don't age here. I am the great-grandmother of your mother, whom I adore so much, and I have been watching over you for some time. Even though you lost her so young, I did gain her here."

Just then my mind is being filled with a vision. I'm the little girl again in the car, Dad is driving, Mum is sitting next to him, and we're all laughing and singing until we start spinning for a split second. I thought it was part of the ride until my mum cried out, "God help us." Just then I see an angel sitting next to me. He raises his wings around me—I feel like I'm in a cloud. There's a loud crashing noise; I peep out to see and there are two angels. One is leaving with my mum. She's smiling, but her body is still in the seat while the other angel is laying it's hands over my dad's head with his eyes closed. Then I hear the door open, and a man grabs me and pulls me out before the vision fades and I'm floating above a hospital room. There's a man hooked up to so many machines. Wait, it's my dad, and the woman standing over him is my mum. She has an angel with her; she's telling him that he will be ok and that his work here isn't done; she loves him and they will meet again, and then she leaves and the vision ends.

"What does all this mean? I don't understand. Why did she have to die?"

Lesous looks at me with a tear running down his cheek. "Nichole, everyone dies in your realm; no one is immune from death, remember. No one truly dies, some come here and some stay there, but not in the physical sense. The veil was spilt a long time ago, and this place was made for all who know me, but not the ones that think they do while spreading hate towards others. I knew everyone before they were born; nothing was hidden from me. I've never sought religion; if I wanted robots, I would have created them. I have seen them grow. I have heard them and watched over them and seen the ones that have turned others away from wanting to know me, making their endless lists of things to do, which is impossible to accomplish without me, having their meetings, which I close my ear to. They think they can move me, that I can be invited into their special place, yet they fail to know that I am omnipresent. They believe their special club makes them elite, above everyone else. I will show you only the truth; I am outside of time so I can be everywhere; I have given my power to a select few to teach and guide them to not judge the world but to bring love. If they don't have love, they don't have me; it's a refinement process and not everyone makes it. They can profess to know me yet walk right by me as a beggar in the street; walk right by me as a stranger in their churches; walk right by me as another child is taken and sold into slavery; a country is running from their land in wars and they close their gates, not welcoming them in or helping them to feel safe and loved. They use my name in their hate towards others based on skin colour, social status, or even sexuality; they judge the flesh of a person instead of loving them and meeting all where they're at and intimately trusting and knowing me. I have never made anyone or anything that I was not pleased with and extremely fond of; my anger only rises when I see ones who say they represent me and speak on my behalf when I was wasn't there and was silent. Like I said, nothing was hidden from me and they will be judged as they judge."

My mind is racing now as I blurt out, "Are you God? Am I dead?"

He smiles and laughs. "No, you're not dead, and I am—that I am. I have many names, some I'm very fond of, in every language and tongue."

I blurt out again, "If you're God, then why is there so much pain in the world? Where are you when this happens? Why are so many hungry and poor? Why all the death with wars and disease?"

"Everyone is given free will; it's gift and they can choose many different paths and the effects of their decisions is passed on through their generations. Some bring blessings, but some bring curses. They have the free will to help a fellow in need or ignore; they can choose healing or hate; they can choose to follow me out of fear or love. There are enough provisions on earth that no one should ever be hungry, but they rape the waters and most of it is thrown away. They invent chemicals to make more fruit or meat, most of which is also thrown away and contaminated and which causes the body to slowly decay. The environment they create is one of their main causes of disease, but the most important reason is what's in their hearts that causes them to not live out a fulfilled life. Their hearts are hardened, they are walking around with a veil on them so they cannot see the beauty and pain around them.

"All get to choose with their own free will. You have your own free will, Nichole. You can also choose. I will never make anyone do anything; if I need something, I will create it. I have someone who is wanting to meet you again. I know this has only answered some of your thoughts. To answer them all, I would have to show you man's error and that will take much longer, and for many of these errors, the ones who made them have renounced them, so they are in the sea of forgetfulness."

He's smiling, and my mind is rolling. He has an answer for everything, but it also makes so much sense. I've been so hurt by religion, and I always thought I'd be dragged before a throne with concrete steps covered with angry angels and a god that was going to send me straight to hell, but this isn't that at all. I actually could get used to this; it's so peaceful here, so calm and lovely, but I do have one quick question.

"Lesous, is this your throne room?"

He laughs. "No, Nichole, this is your great-great-grandmother's and I am her guest."

She laughs too. "My very favoured and welcomed guest, I might add. Nichole, I had so many of the same questions that you have. The world was at war when I was there; it was such a dark place. I left that world from contracting Spanish flu and left behind a small family; my two twin children were only three. Brigette and William went on through life and started families of their own. Brigette married Albert; he was a sailor. They had five children and had many, many years of happiness with eighteen grandchildren. William married Kathleen and had three children. He worked as a carpenter, and one of those children, Pauline, was your grandmother. She had three children; your mother was one of them. Sadly, she died giving birth to the youngest and the eldest died in her sleep before she was three. Your mother was the only surviving child, and she had you and Andrew. So, you see, when I was dying, I was so full of fear about leaving them behind and what would happen to them. Lesous told me that my husband would remarry and all would be well, and I received great peace before I left. So, you see, when we only focus on life through the lens of fear, we accomplish nothing, but when we trust and have peace, well, just look at where I am and you are here with me. I couldn't be happier, my dear, sweet, beautiful girl."

The way she just explained it me makes so much sense, and this place is amazing; I can only feel love here. Did I just think that, really? I feel love, I am loved, I was loved. Just then I feel my body respond in a deep relaxation, one I can't find words to describe. Lesous interrupts my thoughts.

"Nichole, there is someone here who has been waiting to meet you. Are you ready?"

I'm feeling a little weird, as it's not my place to say yes or no to this question and I have no idea which ancient relative I might meet, so I respond with a simple "yes."

In through the oak-framed door walks a beautiful woman. She's wearing a long floral green dress with a cream shawl covering her shoulders. She looks about my age. Her curly long red hair, like mine, is so shiny, it's almost blinding. Wait, just wait a minute— Momma, is that you? As I feel a fountain of tears rising from within me, like my heart will burst. I run over to her. She drops to her knees to embrace me. I put my arms around her shoulders, just bursting. Wait—I'm little again, I'm a child, I'm so tiny. "Oh, my tinker bell, oh, how I've missed you." My entire being is like jelly; I am melting into her. I can smell her fragrance, I can feel her warmth, I can feel her love. I am crying years of tears, soaking her shoulder. "I am here now, I am here, and you are with me. Oh, how I have missed you."

Why am I a child? As soon as I think it, Lesous says, "Because you needed to be this little girl again to be healed. Every part of you has a need, and this part needs this moment. Just relax and embrace your mother's love."

I have been an orphan my whole life. I never believed I was ever loved or even wanted. I feel almost complete for the first time in my life. Just then I feel someone else walk into the room. I look up, and as I do, he drops to his knees and puts his arms around both of us. It's my dad—my dad is here and my mommy. "Our little tinker bell, how beautiful you are." Now I'm beyond jelly, I'm actual water, as I feel like my body is flowing in waves of emotions, some leaving, some returning, I feel so complete; I can actually remember this love—they did, they truly loved me. I never want this to end; can I stay like this forever? All that's running through my mind is voices freaking out in happiness; all doubt and fear is leaving. I no longer care about the whys. I just have these moments of childlike Joy—I finally have love.

Chapter Eleven

I awake and I'm back in the sunroom. I'm back where I started. Everything is the same, except me—I feel different. Did I just dream all of that? Wait, no, I'm wearing different clothes. I'm wearing the clothes in my dream. Was it a dream? I look over, and Lesous and Mathew are sipping their tea, smiling at me as I sit up to correct my posture.

I don't know what's happening. I usually get flooded with anxiety when I come to, but this time it's different. My skin doesn't feel like I have something crawling under it; my stomach isn't knotted and bloated; I feel a completeness without understanding it. Wherever I was, I want to go back. If it was a dream, it was the safest, most amazing dream I've ever had. No one was chasing me or trying to cage me. It was an experience I'll never forget, and the love I had there—oh my—I have never felt such love. It was almost like a liquid penetrating my skin. I feel safe and held, like nothing I have experienced before, and I'm not running or rejecting. What is this?

Lesous wonderfully interrupts my train of thought. "Nichole, you are so much more complete. You were not created to withhold trauma. Let me explain. When something so traumatic happens to you that your psyche cannot handle it, it parts you to protect you; it is your soul splitting. You had a lot of trauma, so many parts, and now you're almost healed and whole. Everyone is different in their healing; you needed to go back to where you got stuck. Now that you have the truth your life will completely change. The world around you will become beautiful again. You won't forget your traumas, but now they will no longer rule over you; you won't have an urge to escape because you're not suppressing anything. Your left brain will ignite with creativity because of this healing. You are free now, and even though life does not come without pain, you will never be alone. I will walk through this with you, and when it's time, you will go back to where I just took you, but I'll explain that more later, as I don't want you to lose focus here.

"You have a lot to do with your new life, and your healing will continue. You're like an onion with many beautiful layers, but an onion in a field, and we just prepared the harvest, but there are still so many onions with many layers to explore and heal. I won't ever leave you, and my patience goes beyond this world. I see beyond the human want and will always give you what you need; I just need you to ask within your own free will. Love is a power not a feeling—always remember that."

The moment he says "love is a power," I get flooded again within my entire body and I'm feeling at peace—I mean total quiet; my head no longer has the voices I knew so well. No one is there. Is this what he means? Were there really so many pieces of me broken? I always thought it was just normal that everyone had those voices. Maybe they do. My neighbours will certainly be happy now, as I won't have to play music so loud to drown them out. I chuckle to myself; I now feel like I don't even know me, but it's not a scared and frightened knowing, more of an exciting one. Is this how I would have felt if trauma did not enter my life and try to destroy me, and if death hadn't chased me? Is this now how I am to live, not being chased by death but now chasing life?

Lesous speaks in a more compassionate but firm tone. "Nichole, please come and sit down. You have one more to meet, the last on the list. His name is Choshek."

I interrupt. "The last? Don't I have more to meet, Lesous? How did my father know that I would meet the ones on our trip together? Are they not ghosts?"

He's smiling. "Nichole, I told your father before he came to me for eternity that this was going to take place. I helped him make this plan for you. If everything had been revealed in the beginning, then there would be more barriers blocking you from reaching your goal, our goal."

Feeling an inner peace and safety of knowing that everything so far I have received has been amazing and beyond words, I respond after taking in a deep breath. "You're right, and I will trust you. Let's meet Choshek. I'm intrigued about why he's the last one."

Lesous, more serious now, says, "I want to prepare you because when you do meet him, you will feel that his energy is familiar to mine. It can feel like mine, but there is a way to test it to see, but I will teach you later because, for now, you will know it is him. Just remember, I am with you and I will not leave you. This is the one your dad spoke about in his first letter, and it is important to know the whole truth. He is the enemy who comes as a friend. He will tempt you back to himself, and it is your free will choice, but again, remember, I am fighting for you and with you. Just quiet your mind and you will hear me. Are you ready, Nichole, to meet Choshek?"

Why do feel like this is not a good idea? I feel it deep within my gut; why? But wait, I have a feeling of warmth surrounding me and love—oh, this is not confusing at all. I am not alone, I can do this, and besides, it's not like I'm going anywhere. It's safe here. Just then Lesous reaches over and touches my forehead and I'm knocked out. I feel like my entire being is being transported through time and space in a rushing motion not like before. Then like a jolt, I'm sitting under a tree—a tree in a desert—and the sky is grey and I see a shadow and the sun trying to pierce these dark clouds. Where am I?

Then a figure sits down beside me; I can feel it but cannot really see, and then a deep voice in proper English, like an old English, speaks, but I cannot hear it audibly. I can only hear it in my mind, and it's so clear and loud.

"Nichole, welcome back. I've missed you. Where have you been?"

Missed me? What does he mean, missed me? "I do not know you?"

Oh, is this one of those from a drunken night whom I forgot? Then he instructs me to walk with him, and my entire being obeys. I can feel him next to me but I cannot see him; it's like my head is stiff, only looking ahead, and my feet are following like they are on autopilot, and then he speaks again.

"Nichole, you have been mine for such a long time, and now I'm here to claim you back. Everything you've just gone through is a lie, and he will deceive you because he only wants to be worshipped and to control you. I am here to bring you back and give you the freedom you so desired. I can make you powerful with gifts beyond your wildest imagination. I can give you the husband of your dreams."

Just then a man appears in front of me. He is truly so dreamy. He goes down on his knees, kissing my feet, yuk. I pull back. I don't want anyone kissing those, and then he disappears. What is this magic? I whisper, "Who are you?" He replies with a confidence. "I knew your father very well, and I can give him back to you—your mother, too, if you like. I can bring you all the desires of you heart. Just come back to me."

Come back to you? I don't even know you. Then a blanket-like feeling comes over me like a veil, and I have felt this way before. I'm remembering a scene from the days I was experimenting with drugs. It's a feeling like ecstasy, like my body is jelly and my mind is not my own. But wait, this feeling I've fought before. I don't want this; I never wanted this. I wanted to escape reality, but my reality now has changed, and just then I take a deep breath and quiet my being, and I can hear a small voice. *It's ok, I'm with you.* I jolt back to reality and tear off the blanket, and then I can see him. He's so handsome; he has wavy blond hair and is so muscular, with a perfect skin complexion, and his smile . . . I feel like I'm floating into him.

I shake my thoughts—NO, I'm not looking for this. Just then I'm floating through the air. There's a lake ahead. I feel like I'm going to crash into it and we do, and we're going so fast; there's no bottom—is there an end? Then, within a flash of light, I'm standing and breathing under water in what looks like an old castle, but I'm underwater and I'm breathing—this isn't real. Then I feel a pull into a room filled with gold and precious stones. The walls are like dark granite, except one wall has a fountain of lava moving upwards, against gravity, and the floor is lava under a sheet of glass, and I look and he's wearing an old black armour suit, and the breastplate is filled with emeralds and sapphires. I look over and see two huge golden chairs like thrones; he is sitting in one and I am swept over and placed in the other next to him. I feel something heavy on my head; I reach up and it feels like a crown. I can't take it off; it is hot, like it's sealing itself to my head. Then in a low, deep tone, he says, "You can be my queen, and we will rule over all the kingdoms together. All of this will be yours; just come and be with me, my love."

I look around, and there are people everywhere cheering on their knees with their hands raised. I can hear them saying, "She's home; she's come back. Hail Choshek." I take a deep breath, and I again hear a small, soft voice. *Call me when you need me and I will bring you back.* Yes, I want to go back. I don't want any of this; it doesn't feel good; it looks so dark. As I say that I look into the corner of the room, and I can see people sniffing white powder from the table, and next to them, I can see people having sex. Then I look at him, and he is not so alluring. He is not good; he just parades as good. I can feel he doesn't have a soul—his eyes are black now, whereas before, they were a sparkling blue. Wait—I can see a reflection in his eyes. I see a man drinking whisky from the bottle, and Choshek is next to him drinking, too, and they're laughing. I hear a small voice.

That is your father, Nichole, when he was in darkness, when he knew Choshek. Come back to me. Wait, I don't want this. I try to stand but can't; I am pinned down in my seat and all I can hear is *Lesous, Lesous, call Lesous*, so I cry out, "Lesous!" and with a bang of light, I see the ceiling open and there he is—there's Lesous with what looks like an army with him. They are so bright, it's blinding in this dark castle. Then Lesous speaks and the ground trembles. All he says is, "She is mine," and just then the crown falls from my head, and Lesous stretches out his hand and I reach for it. He pulls me towards himself.

I can hear Choshek say, "She will be tempted again," and Lesous replies, "She might be, but she will be trained well and learn to defeat you." And then I'm jolted back. I'm back in the sunroom; I'm back with Lesous and Mathew. Mathew is smiling, and Lesous looks at me and says, "Well done, Nichole. Well done."

I am feeling such relief to be back. I never want to go there again. It felt like eternity yet only moments. I fall into Lesous with a hug that feels so safe and protective, and I just have a knowing that I am safe. He has proven that he will protect me, and I trust that he will never leave me. I have so many thoughts coming to mind about the vision of my dad drinking whiskey. I am about to ask Lesous what this means when he responds first.

"Nichole, your father was in such darkness when your mother died. He ran away from everyone, including himself. He was so lost, and Choshek took advantage and tempted him for many years, bringing people into his life that kept him from everything that was good, from everything that would bring healing to his soul. His soul was torn between worlds, drowning in the very thing that caused the accident. When I came to rescue your father, it was an amazing moment. I am very fond of him, and I also had to take him back to meet his enemy so he could see the truth. Everyone has the free will to decide, and Choshek will look endlessly for open doors to manipulate every situation to win the person to himself. He demands nothing at the beginning and then everything after, and keeps people in chains like the one you felt on your head, such a heaviness. But I knew you would you overcome him this time, and there will be more and you will overcome them too. You will be trained to fight and in how to fight for others that are lost in his web of lies and deceit. Always remember the future—you do not know but I do, and your future looks amazing and lovely just like you."

I feel like I am encaged with love. I have no fear of the future or the past in this moment. I could stay forever, and to all the Chosheks of this world, I will challenge you because I am free and I want to stay free.

Mathew is staring into the clouds, daydreaming. "Mathew, are you ok?"

Of course, he looks at me and smiles. He says, "Yes, Nichole, I was just recalling my own experience with Choshek and how I too overcame his desires. He only desired me to serve him; I was never a queen, ha ha, but he did offer for me to be a prince, which of course I denied, and then Lesous came in and saved me."

He smiles at Lesous, and Lesous responds with one simple word, "*Habibi*." Oh, that sounds and feels so nice, whatever it means, and with that we all start laughing.

My mind is so calm, and now I know that my life was not a bad dream, that the nightmares came from my inward life or the moments I lost to time. I'm finding myself and the real truth about where I came from and also how I got here. If I need to have a thought, I can now, calmly, without completely crashing down or ripping apart my entire being, mostly internally. I must say, though, before I go on, that I do somewhat miss some of me; after all, what I thought was my subconscious mind turned out to be broken pieces of me constantly stumbling around, fighting for the position of first place, and mostly overtaking the core part of me to achieve their own goals to survive. I thought they were all selfish and came from the dark cosmos or the dead to torment me to keep me in my deathly self; now I realize they played the memories like a record stuck on a turntable, playing the same tune over and over again, doing whatever was needed to escape, drowning out, trying to delete the traumas of the past and how I got broken and unglued.

I remember one time reading about a culture in which when a bone china ornament is broken, they don't just glue it or throw it away; they actually melt real gold and seal the cracks to make it more valuable than before, believing that the brokenness deserves to be soldered delicately and appreciated. This has always stayed in my mind, as I wanted someone to rescue me and delicately believe that my brokenness deserved to be treated with gold, that I was valuable to someone and deserved to be set apart for completeness, and that love wasn't impossible for me and only set apart for a deserving few. Now I feel more than this; I can feel my completeness, my healing, and I deserve to be healed because now I don't just smell a change in the wind of life—I can actually reach out and touch it, grabbing it with all my senses. I am amazed how I can feel my thoughts now, and I can actually see the world in it's true beauty. I feel like I was blind before, and now beauty and love have washed away the veil from my eyes and my heart. Lesous healed me, and for the first time in my life, I feel worthy of such love; without being able to even explain this, I just know.

Chapter Twelve

There's a chiming sound. Mathew gets up and leaves the room as I stare at Lesous. The warm soothing feeling I feel near him—he radiates peace and calmness; he's so beautiful and perfect. I don't ever want to lose this moment in his presence.

"Lesous, please don't ever leave me. I want you in my life always."

And just then, as he turns around, looking directly in my eyes, I do not shun away, my body is not sinking in shame, and I don't feel the need to run and hide. My mind is completely at peace; then I hear an audible voice, "Nichole, you are so loved and I will never leave or forsake you."

Where did that come from? It was his voice, but he didn't move his lips. I can feel a warm oil cover me again, like it's seeping into my skin, deep, like it's erasing my scars. Just then, in walks Mathew with Andrew, my brother. I leap out the chair to run to him. I want to melt inside him, not literally; I mean, I just want to be so close to him. I have never felt this love before and this safety, but I don't care; I'm no longer scared of it. He's my brother. He almost falls back from my hug, which was not the way I would have imagined this. He starts laughing, which makes me laugh, like uncontrollable laughter. Then I hear Lesous and Mathew laughing too, laughter I've never heard or felt before.

Andrew keeps trying to talk, then holds his breath and manages to blurt out, "The party, the party—I've come to take you to the party."

Oh my, yes, I've never had a party. Actually, the last time I did, it was my eighth birthday, when Mary threw a party for me—my only memory of having one. Then after that my birthday was just another day. Oh, I'm so excited. Lesous grabs my attention.

"Nichole, this is a party for you, a celebration of your life, and everyone will be there. There's a room here, upstairs; it's filled with what you'll need to prepare. We'll wait here while you get ready. It's the red door."

I'm so excited. I get up and run towards the staircase, leaping up two wooden stairs at a time. I reach the top. There are so many doors—ah, the red one on the right. As I breathe in deep and open it, I am blinded with a room full of dresses—some on mannequins, the rest on hangers—which look like they're floating from the ceiling, and the back wall is full of shoes of every colour and style, and bags and accessories. Oh my, it's very overwhelming. Just then, a knock on the door. I answer, "Come in." It's a woman. She appears to be in her forties. She's beautiful with her black hair tied up in a bun. She has such a soft face, a gentle, clear face, and perky pink lips and wide green eyes. She has a tape measure around her neck, and she's carrying a wooden case.

"Hi, Nichole, I'm Margarita. I'm here to assist you to get ready for your party—a party for a princess and that princess is you." She's smiling as she opens the case, which is filled with makeup, perfume, and creams. I'm so blown away. I feel so special, and I also have a deep knowing that I do deserve this. The next few hours feel like minutes flashing by as I try on dress after dress. They're all in my size, and all the shoes fit, too. It's amazing, and finally I'm ready. This one I feel comfortable in, and also I feel beautiful—oh my, did I really just think that about myself? Am I beautiful? Can

I truly feel and believe it is true? It's a shimmering black gown; it's long to the ground; the back is completely open, with a black lace trail; the front goes to my neck and my arms are bare. There are cubic zirconia stones along the hem and the waist. She then opens another door, and it's a room filled with jewellery of every kind of stone and gold. She brings out bracelets to try. I chose an amazing cubic zirconia bracelet with a three-layer band, and drop earrings to match.

"Oh, how I wish they were real diamonds, Margarita."

She laughs and says, "Nichole, everything is real, even the ones on your dress. There is nothing fake here, not in Lesous's house."

I'm in a state of shock. "Oh my, you mean even the ones on my shoes are real?"

She shows me the shoes up close. They are plain black with three stones on the strap around the ankle. They have a small heel, not one to break my neck or pierce an eye—amazing, and to think even my feet are worth so much. I feel priceless. Is this how a real princess feels? My hair is down in all its natural curls as she places a small thin diamond tiara on the top, holding back the waves from my face.

I'm not used to having my hair down. I don't know what she did, but it looks amazing. I look amazing. Did I really just think that? Wow. She hands me a black purse with a single diamond on the clasp surrounded by green emeralds. I am complete. Margarita is not my fairy godmother, because in this story, I made the choices, not like the made-up tale. I feel so amazing. I didn't have one negative inner thought; there was not a single dress that made me feel fat and disgusting. As I look in the mirror, I feel a new confidence. I don't see myself as worn and washed out; I see a new me I never imagined I could be.

As I walk down the stairs, Andrew greets me in a royal blue tuxedo. He looks so handsome; I'm so proud of my brother. He looks at me and says, "Oh, Nichole, you sure are beautiful and you kinda look good too." He's so funny, and still with his comment, I don't have a single doubt or voice telling me negative lies about myself. I just feel so calm and loved. Andrew opens the door, and as I take one look around the room, wanting to remember every smell and glimpse of beauty and love, I walk out the door and the beauty is everlasting.

Lesous and Mathew are by the helicopter, both finely dressed, too, in their tuxedos. Lesous is wearing a white tux with a red sash around his waist and Mathew is also wearing a royal blue tux, and they're smiling at me. I can see the light shine from their teeth as I'm drawn towards them. I feel like I'm walking on air, and I'm totally drug-free; that feeling never felt like this, but it's the only way I can describe it, as I have nothing to compare it to. This is as real as it gets.

I get into the seat, not worried at all about the helmet that could wreck my hair. I know it cannot wreck this moment. I turn to Lesous before I put it on.

"Lesous, what if I mess up, make mistakes, do things that will not please you? Would you leave me?"

He tenderly looks me straight in the eyes and grabs my hand, and as he goes to kiss it, he says, "Nichole, I said I would never leave you. You will learn to trust me, and then you will know that no matter what befalls you in life, I am there with you fighting your battles, together. It's not me you will learn to trust, but it's love that you need to trust and know that you are so worthy of such love. It will take time and you will know all the truth about love and why it is a power, not a feeling. Love never fails."

I know now that he is all I will ever need to not just be free but to really be able to live a full life. I have hope in life now; I will choose to go after this life and learn the real meaning of love. I will try to abandon every fear and to no longer abandon me. I will go after complete healing because the road travelled was nothing but darkness and pain, and now I have hope in a new life, a rebirth, an inner excitement that I've never had before. I just need to not self-sabotage. Ok, this feels like fear. I shake my head back to reality because reality right now is perfect and free.

You can see the city lights from afar, and the trip feels like it is taking minutes to get there. The sky rises, looks amazing and so colourful. How did I not see this before? It's almost like the dark cloud has shifted over the city. Wait, I can see the clouds moving away from us, faster than I have ever seen before. Then Lesous says, "The clouds know the light and they know how to greet."

What does he mean by "the light"? It's getting dark outside; oh well, we're arriving on the rooftop of a high-rise building. You can see a path lit with candles, I think. Mathew looks at me.

"We're here, Nichole. The party's in the penthouse suite, your dad's place, which, by the way, is now also yours and Andrew's."

Oh my, I can't wait to see it. As we walk down the rooftop stair-case through a door into a hallway, which is mirrored wall to wall with red marble floors. It leads us to a golden door, with a statue next to it of a man and woman holding each other—oh and two little children also; how unique.

Andrew opens the door and shouts, "We're here!"

Lesous holds my hand and guides me in. There must be over a hundred people here or more. They're all clapping; some look like they're crying, wiping their eyes. As he guides me through, down a couple of stairs, people start walking towards me, introducing themselves. I'm never going to remember all their names; then Lesous interrupts my thoughts.

"Nichole, your dad set up many organizations, such as shelters and retreats to help heal people from trauma, which is the main cause of their addictions. The head people of those organizations are here. There's also a team I want you to meet; they worked close with your dad, rescuing children from private mines where they were imprisoned to be sold as slaves. They will guide you through all the wonder that has been achieved on another day. We will do that later, as this is just a meet and greet and everyone is so excited to just meet you. And of course, your family is here. Everyone here is family, not just blood; you're surrounded by people who will always be with you no matter what."

I see Mr. Pathfree walking towards us. He has a golden laptop open. I greet him. "Hello again, Mr. Pathfree." He smiles at me and says, "Please, call me Elias. I am a friend whom you will come to rely on, I'm sure. Besides, looking after finances and legal dramas is my speciality, especially when I fight for truth." This makes me smile and feel safe knowing I have someone else that will fight for me in the legal system. I mean, I remember when I was young and I was up against an assault charge on another girl and we were going to court. The lawyer I had then reminds me of Elias. My lawyer then understood why I had the fight; it was not because I was angry, but because I was a walking time bomb waiting to explode. I was fourteen and she was sixteen, and I remember before the last blow to her head, my hand was stopped in mid-air. Something was holding it back and that freaked me out and still does, looking back. It's also a deep regret of mine. I must find her and apologize. She must know that she did nothing wrong; it could have been anyone that day and sadly it was her. I found out later from the police that if I had hit her one more time in the head, I could have permanently blinded her. Yes, I must seek her out to apologize. I feel a deep inner conviction to make things right.

Taking a deep breath, I watch Elias as he turns the laptop screen to Lesous, who touches it, then he says, "It's complete, Nichole. Everything we discussed is now yours. I'll come by tomorrow and discuss it further."

He smiles and excuses himself, saying, "I still have a few rough edges to crease out, but no worries. The transfer of funds is done and the ten million is now in an account in just your name. I'll see you tomorrow, Nichole, and enjoy this evening. By the way, you look absolutely beautiful."

I completely forgot. I forgot about the money; it all seems so little of importance compared to the way I feel now. Can you really put a price on the value of healing? I didn't have to pay someone $100 an hour to vent. Could you imagine how much that would have cost me with this past week? The freedom and peace I have now, you can't buy, and I certainly would recommend this path. Oh my, there's a huge feast of food, people dancing; everyone's so happy—I'm so happy. I'm finally happy and free. I must go now and enjoy this moment. I'll write again soon to tell you all what happened next, as this really is just the beginning of an adventure that will never end.

Afterword

I have left this place for me to share with you some of my writings that I made for a group I created to help people fall in love with themselves. It was the biggest part of my journey. I hope you find them helpful and you can feel my heart in every word. Thank you for enjoying this journey with me, and I look forward to seeing you in the second book, which I have already started writing. So, here goes.

Love . . . what IS Love?

Love can be a word that people have thrown around,
doesn't have meaning when it comes from a clown

Love can be the climax
Word that is said in passion till compassion isn't heard

Love can be a strive to stay Alive
Looking for the drive but . . .
There's no Love inside a beehive

Inside Me

Love oneself, how can that be
When I look in the mirror and all I see is a different me I
don't wanna be . . .

Love others—with what, I ask
When all I do is wear a mask
Seeking them to be the one without a gun

Love . . . what is Love?

Love is kind with one mind

Love is Patient with endurance to just be Free

Love is Compassion to Really see Me

Love is Long suffering . . . waiting through locked gates,
searching for the key to release me

Love is Tender and touches Deep within

Love is Forgiving the Mess I am in

Love is a Tsunami crashing my rocks to melt me to sand
undoing my locks

Love is never found in just one man

Love is deeper where there is No fault
It's a unity with many not in a locked vault

Love is a Deep kiss from within my soul

Love covers me like a blanket without any holes

Love is an oil which saturated my skin
When I try to wipe it off it goes Deep within

Love is a gift which keeps giving
Not for the dead but for the Living

So when I seek Love and to Love myself
My journey brought me to this conclusion
Which is the truth not confusion

The Key which opens Every lock is to forgive yourself for all
the time lost
No one can fill you, it's a spiritual tool to seek on the path to
the way and the truth

The Crumbs of Pain

Pain comes in many forms, physical, emotional, and it has many roots. Some are like a suffocating weed, which feels like a constant tug around your throat, and others manifesting in the body like huge warnings signs that the ship is gonna hit rocks. It comes from what people say and do, or the lack of what they say and do. When someone says they love you or someone is supposed to, but the body doesn't feel a safe place to be. When someone who says they love you takes your innocence away and pretends like nothing bad ever happened and you're left with an emptiness, a confusion of what love is, then a relationship you try to seek but never find because you aren't aware of what healthy looks like, you are just running from what pain looks like.

Many are walking around with a billboard in front of them—an image to the world that they're safe, happy, and fun, but after time, when the cardboard gets wet and starts to breakdown, you see their true self and the slime they really are, slime because it's melting, falling apart, leaving traces on the floor as it walks and talks, and all you're left with is stains on your body and you're stuck in places inside that you never venture to understand exist. The lies, the lies they hide behind are like an old torn-down building that's protected by heritage, but we all know it needs to be taken away. But it's still there, a reminder of the past for the future to see, but what if, what if as we learn to fall in love with ourselves, we learn that we are worthy to be loved and we challenge ourselves to see deep inside, to see the hidden places that we run from only to find we have younger ones of ourselves that we can rescue, that we can listen too, and heal? The chains inside fall off and we can smash all the mirrors of doubt, fear, and rejection; we can start living a life we truly desire instead of the hopelessness we've come to believe is our reality.

In my journey in the onion field, I've uncovered so many layers upon layers, and really, they're not as scary as I thought; they're just layers of lies, ones I've believed about myself and as I learn to love myself the inside heals, and as I'm learning to love my body, that it is safe, I'm becoming more connected. And with this connection, I can now sit in the quiet, where I couldn't before because the quiet was too much of a challenge. I've overcome so much in life and buried so much. I no longer want an internal grave yard; I want an internal garden. Filled with flowers of every kind, with an oasis of peace, not because someone told me I deserve it but because I now know I do.

Letting go of the past is different than denying its existence. Facing it has been one of the hardest things I've ever had to do, but worth every tear because now my tears are washing away the pain. My body is healing because it's being heard and I have learned to laugh again, truly laugh, and also I can be still, even in the mist of a storm. I can stand still . . . No storm will take you out; no human can . . . You can stand your ground and fight for your healing because You Are Worth It. ❤❤❤

They Said . . .

They said I was broken; they said I was strong. They said I was hard and I've been that way too long. They said I should cry and then asked me why . . . Have you had people say things about you that you don't agree with, and more often they seem contradictory? Why is it that we care what others think when they're often the ones that don't have their own lives put together, they don't have lives that one would want? . . . People mirror-reflect from their subconscious, which is programmed with what the world and the people in it should be. It's an important part of healing to not self-reflect on what others are doing, which can often only avoid going deep within yourself. Going deep can be painful or challenging; we can't undo our thinking by just saying positive affirmations when your subconscious is programmed otherwise, because that just creates an inner war.

For the first seven years of our life, we're like little computer boards observing our surroundings, watching, and mimicking what others do and believe, whatever they tell us. If you had a negative experience or harmful one, then without knowing it, you grow up either the victim or believe the world wants to hurt you and that your body is not a safe place to be. So without deep healing, you're just sticking Band Aids on your pain and your belief systems. You can have an awakening and believe the world around you will help and heal you until you stumble and realize that even that is temporal. . . . So why is it so important to go deep for healing and not just "get over it" (which, by the way, is the worst thing you can ever say to someone)? In my experience, going deep is painful but not as painful as the lie I believed that if I ever opened that door, I would be locked in. No, I opened the doors of pain and realized that fear was its guardian and I wanted healing because

I deserve it. When I passed fear, like stepping on a bug, and faced my past, I had to turn a key—the key was forgiveness. Not just for them but for me; I wasn't letting them off the hook; I was handing them over to a greater power than myself and then the miracles started to happen. I was free, the pain wasn't there anymore, and that monster behind the door was just another wounded victim themselves. So, through my own journey of healing I can honestly say that instead of having those monsters behind doors keeping you in fear's reach, you have to stand your ground and fight, and when you do, you realize you're not struggling with fear; you're just giving it a gentle blow and watching it wither away. . . .

The journey through healing isn't for anyone, it's a choice—a choice to stay in the closet, or to escape to See, Feel, Smell, Taste, and fully experience Life.

Love to all and, remember, Loving yourself comes from taking the power back from the ones that you believe deep inside still have you in chains. When you realize those chains are just paper-clips, they're easy to break.

What Is Time . . .

Time is an interesting conversation. Time flies so fast unless you're going through something deep; then it drags its heels. Time . . . so many want and take it when it's yours, and then it's like their dust blowing in the wind. Time . . . heals and helps develop a deeper meaning to life which is the age of time . . . time . . . Some people are begging for more whilst others are wishing it away . . . time . . . Life is time, a clock forever ticking, forever sticking, but . . . it's time we learn to understand. Time, respect other people's and cherish our own. Getting stuck in time is understandably the worst pain, but then there's that one special soul that grabs your hand as your falling and lifts you up back to life. There's that one precious soul that listens to your heart and models a life of how love is truly perfected. There's that one precious soul that rips apart words like Enjoy and leaves Joy. There's always that one precious person, no matter how long or little they were in your life; there are still moments you can see with unclouded vision; there was a reason. Time is an interesting conversation. Don't waste it; don't walk over others that give it. And learn to Fly, because you're worth it and so are they . . . so am I. I truly thank those that gave and give me their time. 💜💜💜💜

Letting People In

Interesting concept for those that have been burnt before, but through my own experience not letting people in (something I did till my thirties) was more detrimental to building relationships with friends than it was keeping them out. I've spent years learning how to be more vulnerable (haven't mastered it yet) when letting people in, but I do find that maybe I'm not suppose too . . . maybe it's for only a certain few. Maybe my role in this life is to be a pillar of strength. Many of us have many faces. Our roles in life give us so many . . . a wife, mother, daughter, sister, aunt, cousin, friend, and even foe. To be honest, it can be exhausting if you're not in a place of healing and knowing your worth in those said roles. So, vulnerability doesn't mean you disclose everything; it doesn't mean you have to trust everyone (trust is earned), but it does mean you have the strength and wisdom to choose and decide, do I show a role or show my soul? I'm always searching for the better side of me, and maybe then I'll be able to see the world as it truly is. To me, it's a very worthwhile adventure. Remember, only a select few truly know me. I don't share much, but when I do, I know it's worth it. Be cautious, be vulnerable, be humble, be wise, but most importantly be You and find the best of you, always sampling the beauty this world does offer us. When you seek, you shall find.

Judging

The saying "Don't judge me till you walk a day in my shoes," well . . . I walk through life with Doc Martens on, with steel toecaps, not flip flops, so if you wonder about me stubbing my toes, then don't. I analyze every decision, and the ones I don't, I love more. Being in love with life is a treasure I protect, not the martyring because of someone's thoughts, feelings, or corrections that they think my life should be. Real people will love you where you're at, and if you fall, they'll give you their hand to pick you up and remind you what it is to laugh again. Life is to be chased; go after it with Passion and Love. Don't live with regrets, allowing it to pass you by. We live once so LIVE IT and LOVE IT, and in the end, you won't just be holding your heart but the hearts of many that have enjoyed it with you. Have a Fabulous, Amazing, Adventurous Life and Always be surrounded with Love like a blanket without any holes. xoxo

Love Every Single Part of Your Body

Most of us are not friends with our bodies. You must be thinking, "Ok where's Zoe going with this one?" Ha ha. But seriously, hear me out. Let me paint a picture of the invisible enemy. As a child abused, your body wasn't safe, so you hid from it. As a child, a separation in your family caused deep pain. As a child, a parent was lost to you and you couldn't run away from the pain. Maybe a sickness made you yearn for a different body; maybe the leftover scars and many other examples. So, this child grows up with the distorted vision of this body is not good. I use the word child, because for most truths, it begins early. This earth suit contains pain and you are stuck in it. You can try to run away from it, pushing it through miles of running and hours at the gym; you can starve it or over-feed it and never feel one with it; you can compare it to other suits, wanting what theirs looks like, all the more hating your own, even the things on your body, like hair, facial hair, chest hair, underarm hair, private hair—all an annoyance—hating your facial features, hating your legs and wanting them to hide. You get the point.

But what if we became friends with our bodies? What if we went on a path of deep forgiveness for ourselves and the way we feel about our bodies, and a deep forgiveness of others for how they've also added to the hate of our bodies? So instead of hiding or smashing mirrors, we start to investigate our bodies, make a decision to learn from our bodies. The nervous system is amazing, as it sends the thoughts throughout our body to our brains, even what we think of it. If we think fat, our bodies only know to store fat; if we feel sad, we only know to comfort eat or starve, which makes us reject our bodies more. But studies have been done to show the connection of the eyes to what we eat. Blindfolded, the person listens more to the stomach and stops when they're full. Amazing.

Feeding our bodies through emotions, we all know, isn't healthy; that's why diets don't work. Instead, we look at a sandwich, for example, and instead of picking at it or woofing it down, we close our eyes and listen to our stomach. When we open our eyes, again, amazingly, there's some left.

Then we can also look at the skin—it's colour, texture, how it stretches and heals, how the hairs protect it from sun and dust, also keeps it warm. Look in a mirror with a renewed mindset of exploring your body, write down what you see, not what you feel but what you see; then close your eyes and put your hands slowly over your body and use your mind to think about your body, and it's amazing how the thoughts instantly change. Write those down, do a comparison, make friends with your body, check out the digestive system, do a short study on the ways the body functions, how even the blood works—because anytime we make a new friend, we automatically want to learn everything about that friend, but this time, the friend is your own body. Let your soul explore it in a different way.

Your body is not the enemy. What others have done to you or how you have punished your body—it's time to stop, do a complete turnaround, and start loving your body. Fall in love with your body, its uniqueness, its beauty, its ability to heal, to function and to attract. It doesn't matter about yesterday; what matters is now. Change the way you see yourself, and within days, you will start to notice that other people are seeing you different too; when we start to love within our souls and body, we let out a vibrant glow that others see, and when they ask you, "What's new?" you can say with a huge smile, "ME!" ❤❤ Make the change within and fall in love so deeply with yourself that it will pour out to others freely. ❤❤❤

Breaking the chains . . .

How do we heal from hurts and pains of the past when we realize we never understood what love was, only what we'd been taught—that it brings some kind of false security, a feeling, not a power? Going on a self-discovery journey to find out what love Really is . . . well, that's the freedom. Imagine with me; imagine a string filled with beads. Each bead represents a past relationship, friendship, family member, or even yourself. Each bead holds onto a pain, a rejection, a trauma, a betrayal, soul wounds, and flesh wounds; now, imagine the beads are getting pretty heavy as we age through life, forgetting this necklace we're wearing but feeling the weight of it, then moving forward into another relationship, friendship, etc., wearing this heavy yoke around our neck like we're cattle, until you start to realize that the past can't be buried or forgotten—it needs to be ripped off, unpacked, and dealt with. We don't need a security blanket giving us false security; forgiving those that hurt you, even yourself, brings freedom because they're no longer around your neck; they've turned into beautiful pearls, from darkness to light. Then we can appreciate our past, as it made us who we are, but that doesn't happen until you start loving yourself, and having the ability to laugh at the past instead of being in a cave with it. . . . Love yourself because, baby, you're Worth it. You are already Beautiful; you are a survivor; you are already free; you just need to take away the invisible things that hold you down. So, choose to be free and to not push down the past, thinking it doesn't matter, because it does. The past refines you; it doesn't define you. Be Free. Love yourself, because even when you don't feel it, You are loved. Love is a power, not an emotion. ❤️ ❤️ Sending waves of love to you all. ❤️ ❤️ ❤️

A Final Note

Sometimes it's healthy to step aside and allow the ride to pass; there is always another one, and maybe that one wasn't fast enough, exciting enough, or challenging enough for you, because you are so unique, creative, and able to see what others are blind to. Maybe the ride you're waiting for is perfectly already awaiting You, waiting for you to be who you need to be, not perfecting but deflecting all the cages that have been holding you back. The ride of life has a one-way ticket, and you must know the ticket you're holding. We all ride it together but get off it alone.

Printed in Canada